A MESSAGE FROM THE E

Dear Reader,

I had to shut out the world to finish editing this short story collection.

Neighbours became concerned.

Banged on my door.

My kidnappers had taken me down to the cellar with a copy of the book.

I read it again and again, and over again...

It made my torture and captivity so bearable that I was annoyed when the Marines rescued me.

Sincerely yours,

χ

The Editor-in-Chief*

READERS CIRCLE OF AVENUE PARK

P.S. Twisted Tales is mixed-fruit jam for the soul. Laugh, cry, dwell deep and sigh. Enjoy!

**Note from the assistant to the assistant to The Editor-in-Chief, "Alas, our esteemed E-in-C has gone into hiding with a dog-eared copy of Twisted Tales; as such his (or her) identity remains a secret. Only splendid reviews from readers like you might bring him (or her) back into the sunlight."*

TWISTED TALES

15 Literary Lies & Epic Yarns

Edited By

READERS CIRCLE OF AVENUE PARK

ACKNOWLEDGMENTS

Our gratitude is extended to the editorial team—and most of all the readers of READERS CIRCLE OF AVENUE PARK for their untiring efforts in curating this unique short story anthology. It was a global effort, literally, with authors contributing across exhausting time zones that extended from Africa, Europe, America and Asia.

To retain this distinctive international flavour (or 'flavour') each story is in the English style of its author, so some stories are in British English, some in American, and some reflect the jargon of a region.

The views and opinions expressed in this literary work are those of the author(s) and do not necessarily reflect the views or opinions of the READERS CIRCLE OF AVENUE PARK editorial team.

Cover artwork by M.J. Fine

Picture Credits: Creative Commons/CCO Pixabay

All the characters, companies, and organisations in this book are fictitious, and any resemblance to actual persons, living or dead, is purely coincidental.

The Authors have asserted their rights under the Copyright, Designs and Patents Act 1988 to be identified as the authors of this work.

First published by

ISBN 978-1-326-65481-8

ReadersAvenuePark.com

@ReadersAvePark

Hashtag #RCAP

CONTENTS

A MAN WALKS OUT OF A BAR

J. Mayerson Brown

I checked in at the front desk then headed straight to the bar. As my eyes adjusted to the dim lighting, I looked for a place to sit. I didn't care where as long as I had a cold beer in my hand in the next two minutes. I licked my dry lips and scanned the room. It was then that her hair caught my eye. Dark red, auburn, I think. And it cascaded down her back in curly waves. As I stood staring, she shifted, and her skirt rose just enough to share a glimpse of pale, smooth skin. The empty stool next to her beckoned.

I searched for a different seat. Not that I didn't want to sit next to her. I did. I just knew I shouldn't . . .

It wasn't a good time for me. My wife and I were in counseling. We'd been seeing the therapist for a few weeks, and I already wanted to quit. He was a pompous asshole with an irritating laugh that made me want to punch him in the face. But he was good at what he did, and I was willing to do anything to make things right.

Jill and I had been together ever since our sophomore year at Berkeley. Back then we both were pot-smoking, Bush-hating, liberals. We held everyone who didn't think the way we did in disdain. It's very romantic when you're in your twenties to believe your parents are idiots, especially when you're learning nothing but politically correct bullshit from professors who had spent their youths protesting the war in Vietnam. Jill and I reveled in that - letting our parents spend their hard-earned money on our tuition and coed housing while we listened to lectures about the evils of capitalism.

Eventually we grew up. We abandoned our contempt of the upper class in favor of fine wine, new cars, and summer vacations. A few friends dumped us because of it, but we were like, "screw them." We were living the dream - condo in Santa Monica overlooking the Pacific, expensive restaurants, Italian sheets. Our so-called friends could judge all they wanted. We were working our asses off, and that entitled us to spend our money however we chose.

Time marched on, as it always does, and we hit forty. Our parents were getting old. Our friends were getting divorced. Our jobs were getting mundane. And we started to question our decision not to have kids.

One night we were at dinner with another couple. I looked at Jill, still beautiful, but distant, preoccupied, practically a stranger. And I thought to myself *How did we get here?*

I strayed first. On a business trip. A couple of nights, that was it. Jill was devastated, and I wished I had sucked up the guilt and never told her. Hurt gave way to anger, and she became nasty. Then she withdrew. I groveled and cried and begged her to forgive me. Nothing worked, that was until she had an affair. I was relieved. Jill had evened the score, and I would be the epitome of understanding and reason. She did it to get back at me, and I was okay with that. But then she said she was in love with the guy. Jesus Christ, why couldn't women be more like men?

We separated, and I stood by while my wife fucked some other guy. I suffered for three months. The day she called and said she wanted to work things out was the happiest day of my life. She insisted we go to therapy, and of course I agreed . . .

The bar was teeming with the after-work crowd, and the only available seat was next to the red hair.

"Shit."

It was July in Dallas - over ninety degrees with humidity that felt like a hot, wet towel wrapped around me. I walked up to the empty stool and stood beside it, angling myself so I wouldn't, couldn't, see her face. The bartender asked what I was drinking. I ordered a Guinness. He held the glass at a forty-five degree angle and allowed the dark liquid to flow down the side.

The bartender placed my beer on a white napkin in front of me. My mouth felt dry as sawdust. Keeping my back to the red hair, I sat on the stool and picked up the glass.

"I'm so sorry, but would you mind not sitting there?"

I turned. Damned if her face didn't surpass the hair. "Excuse me?"

Her brown eyes opened wide, and she gave me an apologetic smile. "I'm, well, I'm waiting for someone. He should be here any minute."

Her explanation kind of annoyed me. I took a drink of my beer and wiped the foam off my upper lip with the back of my hand.

"Tell you what," I said. My tone was nice, not obnoxious, because I'm that kind of a guy. "I'm just having the one, so would it be okay if I sat here until your friend arrives?"

"Oh, um, I guess so." She raised a shoulder in a way that was girlish, cute. She looked to be in her late twenties, give or take. She had fair skin with a few freckles sprinkled across her nose.

The girl glanced at her cell. "He's a half hour late."

I didn't respond. None of my business if she was dating a jerk. I leaned on my elbows and drank.

The guy on the other side of the girl got up and left. I turned toward her. "You think you could hold that seat for your friend? I'd like to order one more."

"Sure, that's fine."

"Thanks." I waved at the bartender and pointed to my empty glass.

I drank my second beer more slowly. It felt good going down. I took out my phone and scrolled through my emails, deleting most of them. Then something bumped my arm.

"I'm sorry," the girl said. She was putting her purse over her shoulder.

"You're leaving?" I looked past her and saw the stool was still empty.

Her eyes drifted toward the door. "Pretty sure he isn't coming."

"Wait," I said.

She gave me a curious look.

"You're not gonna give up that easy, are you?"

"What do you mean?"

"You said he's a half-hour late. Give the guy a break. Maybe he's stuck in a traffic." I didn't give a shit about the other guy. What the hell was I doing?

She shook her head. "He's not coming."

I felt sorry for her. "Well, doesn't have to be a total loss. I'll buy you a drink." I held my breath. Jill's affair had destroyed my ego. Therapy made me vulnerable. Any rejection, even from a stranger, would hurt.

The girl toyed with a few strands of hair, twirling her fingers beside the soft skin behind her ear. "Well, I guess one drink is okay." She sat back down.

"All right then." I signaled the bartender. "What'll you have?"

"Um," she twisted her mouth in thought. "Vodka soda, please."

Without expression, the bartender said, "Got ID?"

The girl laughed. "Are you kidding? I'm thirty-one."

"Sorry. It's my job."

When she realized he was serious, she pulled out her license and showed it to him. She did look awfully young.

"Are you really thirty-one?" I asked as the bartender made her drink.

"Do you want to see my ID, too?" She gave me a smile, wrinkling her nose.

"No," I said, although I sort of did.

The bartender put the vodka soda in front of her. She picked it up and took two sips. "Mmm, tastes good." She gave me a sidelong glance. "What's your name?"

"Mitch." The minute I said it, I wished I had made one up. "Yours?"

"Diana."

We smiled absently at one another. Silence. I looked at her hands wrapped around her glass. They were small with short nails painted dark blue. I was used to Jill's nails - long and always red.

"The guy I was waiting for," Diana said, breaking the awkward silence. "It was a, um, just an online thing, so really no big deal. My boyfriend, well, I mean my ex-boyfriend, moved away, and I've been . . ."

I sort of stopped listening. Her voice danced around my ears as I watched her talk, nodding as if I were paying attention. All I really wanted was to look at her as she sipped her drink with full, wet lips and picked cashews out of the bowl of nuts. I didn't want a connection. At least I didn't want to want one.

"I love cashews," she said, pushing the other nuts out of the way with her index finger.

"I see that." I reached for the bowl of nuts to my left and put it in front of her.

"Anyway," Diana said, licking salt from her fingers, "my friends talked me into trying online dating. This is my first no-show."

"No kidding? I'd think it would happen all the time."

She looked at me straight on. "That's mean."

I back peddled. "No, wait, I said it wrong. It's just that guys are lazy assholes when there's nothing at stake."

She eyed me as if doubting my sincerity. "Really?"

"Really. You've never actually met this guy, right?"

"Yeah, so?"

"So what does he care? Maybe he decided to stay home and watch TV. Maybe something better came up." I spoke with authority, as if I were giving her a little insight into the male mind.

A smile played at the corners of her mouth. "Cynical, aren't we?"

I took a drink of my beer. "Life will do that to you."

She scratched the back of her neck, under the red hair. "Have you tried it?" she asked

"Tried what?"

"Online dating."

I choked. "Um, no."

"Maybe you should."

"Maybe I shouldn't." I shifted in my seat. "I'm married."

"Oh. Where's your ring?"

I looked at my left hand. I'd taken my wedding band off when Jill and I separated. Jill had done the same. I sure as hell wasn't going to put mine back on until she did. I cracked my knuckles. "It's complicated."

Diana pursed her lips. "I'll bet it is."

"Now you're sounding cynical."

"Life will do that to you."

I busted up. She was fucking adorable.

"So you're thirty-one and single," I said. "Tick-tock."

She slugged my arm hard, and the pain felt great.

"What? It's a joke."

"Not really," she said. "It's hardly funny that I stuck with the same guy all through college and law school, and then he dumps me."

"You're a lawyer?"

"I am."

I studied her more closely. "You don't look like a lawyer."

She leaned back with an appraising gaze. "What should a lawyer look like?"

"I don't know, conservative. Brooks Brothers suit." I took a cashew and popped it in my mouth. "Definitely not blue nail polish."

Diana gave me another one of her cute, wrinkly nosed smiles. "Yeah, the nail polish throws everyone off. But I do wear a proper suit when I'm in trial."

I tried to picture her in court, standing in front of a judge. A big, tough Texas judge. And my attraction to her intensified. "I'm an accountant," I said.

"I figured."

"You figured? What's that mean?"

Diana chuckled. "Just your look. Very CPA, all crisp white shirt, clean shave, shiny shoes. You're sort of a sexy, nerdy numbers guy."

"Nerdy?"

"Sexy nerdy. It's a compliment, actually. Totally my type."

I rubbed my forehead. She was killing me. My defenses were approaching zero. Classic scumbag cliché - married man on a business trip picking up some girl in a bar. Four days ago I was pledging fidelity to my wife. What the hell was wrong with me?

"Are you staying here in the hotel?" Diana asked.

Say no say no say no . . . "Yep."

She raised a shoulder, and I wondered if she was toying with me.

"Why do you ask?"

She gave me a look that said "*you know why,*" and I weighed my options. I felt like the tables had turned, and now she was leading the way. My offer to buy her a drink had been so transparent, I might as well have come right out and asked her up to my room. But she went from being young and cute to smart and intriguing, a combination I found irresistible.

I swallowed. "Are you suggesting something?"

Diana sipped her drink. "I don't know. Maybe."

I felt a stirring in my groin. I scratched my chin and tried to ignore the proverbial angel and devil who had just popped up on my shoulders:

ANGEL: "What are you doing? Get away now! You'll regret it. Haven't you learned your lesson?"

DEVIL: "Do it! Just do it and don't tell this time. She's practically handing it to you on a silver platter!"

ANGEL: "Be strong. You're making progress. Jill's finally starting to trust you again!"

DEVIL: "What are you waiting for? Quit overthinking! She's giving it away!"

The angel and devil battled it out, and Diana's unspoken offer lingered. I felt my jaw twitch.

"Tell you what," Diana said, interrupting the tug of war going on in my head. "I need to use the restroom. If you're here when I get back, great. If not, then thanks for the drink."

I watched her walk through the lounge, her red hair swaying with each step, and disappear into the lobby.

"Another Guinness?" The bartender's voice startled me.

I turned. "No. Just the check."

I stood up. I waited. Everything was riding on how quickly I paid the bill. I would play the game. If I didn't get out before she returned, I'd have no choice but to take her upstairs. The decision wasn't mine to make anymore. I relinquished control to chance, to a twist of fate. The bartender handed me a bill. I picked it up. I glanced at it. Cash or credit card? I rarely carried cash, but I had some on me. A sign. I put down two twenties. Generous tip. Done. Leave. I slid the money under the bowl of nuts and turned around.

"You're still here," Diana said.

Man, she was fast. Jill always spent at least ten minutes in the bathroom.

I took a deep breath. "I am."

Diana gave me shy smile. “Okay then.”

My heart raced. Beads of sweat formed on the back of my neck. Conflict, ambivalence - my body and my brain were parting ways. Every fiber of me wanted to be naked with Diana, to feel her skin, her hair, her lips. And I had let fate decide, because I was a weak and indecisive schmuck. No wonder Jill had fallen in love with somebody else.

“You look really nervous,” Diana said.

“Me? No, I’m not. Are you?”

Another game. If she said she was nervous, I’d have my out.

“Uhh,” she said. “Should I be?”

Typical, evasive answer. Why did women always do that?

“Absolutely not.”

“That’s a relief.” She tucked her purse under her arm. “Lead the way.”

I forced my breathing to slow down. I placed my hand on the small of her back and started guiding her toward the exit. We wound our way between tables and chairs, waitresses carrying cocktails on trays, patrons entering and leaving.

“Diana!”

We halted. A young man, practically a kid, stood in front of us, sweaty and disheveled, his tie crooked.

"Oh my God," the kid said. "I can't believe you're still here. I'm such an idiot. I went to the Marriott, and I was waiting for you there for like an hour. Then I checked my messages and remembered we'd changed the plan to meet here. I'm really sorry!"

"You're Troy?" Diana said.

I took a step back. I felt like I had gone from host to unwelcome guest.

"Yes." Troy blinked, his eyebrows raised behind black framed glasses. "That's me."

"You don't look anything like your picture."

"Yeah, it's old. I'm sorry."

"That's okay," Diana said. "I, well, I was . . ." she glanced over her shoulder at me as if she had no idea what to do.

Troy frowned in confusion. "Is there, um, did I . . ."

The man in me stepped forward. "You owe me a favor, buddy."

"I do?" Troy asked.

"He does?" Diana said.

"Sure. I told her not to give up so fast. That maybe you were late for a reason. And as it turns out, you were. Lousy reason, but still believable." I looked Troy in the eye and gave him a good-natured squeeze on the shoulder. "Anyway," I said, turning to

Diana. "Enjoyed chatting with you. Good luck with your, um, the trial."

Diana raised her chin. "Right. Thanks."

"Troy," I said, offering my hand. "Nice to meet you. And a word of advice?"

"Yes sir?"

Jesus. Sir?

"Try not to keep a girl waiting, especially a pretty one like Diana."

Troy's Adam's apple slid up and down his neck. He ran a hand through his hair and grinned. "Right. Thanks."

"Have a good one." I walked out with all the nonchalance I could muster and stopped on the other side of the wall. Troy was a loud talker.

"I'm so glad you didn't leave. I know we were just going to meet for a drink, but it's almost eight. Are you hungry?"

"Famished."

"Me too. What's your favorite? Italian, Chinese? What about sushi?"

"I love sushi."

I could hear the smile in Diana's voice. I watched them head toward the front door of the hotel. Then Diana looked back, as if she knew I would be there still. She said something to Troy. He nodded. She came toward me.

"Change your mind?" I asked.

Diana laughed. "Thanks for making that so easy."

"What do you mean? It was the truth."

Her smile sparkled. "I guess it was." She planted a quick kiss on my cheek. "You're a good guy. Sort of."

I rolled my eyes. "Yeah, sort of. Hey, have fun with Troy. He seems nice."

"I know, right? And he's pretty cute, don't you think?"

"Well," I said, "that's not something men like to comment on, but I guess so. Maybe kinda sexy-nerdy."

"Exactly."

I watched her rejoin Troy. The pair walked side by side, talking as they made their way across the lobby, through the double doors, and out onto the street.

*****

ABOUT THE AUTHOR

JULIE MAYERSON BROWN *lives just outside of Los Angeles with her family, three dogs, and hundreds of wild peacocks. She has been writing and publishing humorous essays ever since quitting a* *decently paying job to stay home and take care of two sons and lots of pets. Her first novel,* ***The Long Dance Home****, was published in 2013 by Mischievous Muse Press.*

Julie usually can be found in one of the quiet corners of her local library where she writes and rewrites and searches for her next dog. She sees a story every time she opens her eyes.

Among her favorite quotes: "I would rather be attacked than unnoticed. For the worst thing you can do to an author is to be silent as to his works." – Samuel Johnson

ACTIVE VS. PASSIVE

Anita Kovacevic

This was simply not my day. I had travelled to the city for job interviews (don't ask—only maybes, nothing promising), and I'd just missed my bus home. The ride back would take three hours, and the next bus was in an hour. Almost all of my money was gone, barely covering the return bus fare, leaving me with just enough for this no-good, chocolate-covered donut which was now soothing my unemployment stress and lulling me into believing the best. I descended the steps next to the river bridge, and strolled along the cobbled path. It was empty, working hours still in progress for the blessed/cursed employed and schoolkids. I liked the quiet, with the city noises in the background reminding me of reality.

A big manmade stone in my path would serve well to relax. The job hunt, family finances gripping tighter than an 18th-century corset, kids sick and hubby laid off … talk about a headache, right?

The stone was not empty. There was a book on it. I looked around for a possible owner. Nobody. Wiping the donut grease off my hand with a mother's must-have—a wet hankie—I let curiosity shorten my wait.

It was not a book. It was a leather bound diary. The letters were so neat they appeared printed from a slight distance. I swallowed my embarrassment like a pill, read a passage, then skimmed through, my heartbeat gaining speed at the words. I unbuttoned my jacket a bit. Air grew thicker, my heart louder, palms sweating.

'Peter is unhappy. John is not around to talk to him man-to-man, and he won't ever be back. Damned plane crash! Peter is only ten. I don't know what to do. He won't talk to me. His friends... Nobody knows why. 'Moody preteens,' teachers said. My boy is pale, distant, quiet... I have to do something. Have to get back to work now. Think about this later.'

The city noise faded in the distance. All I could now hear in my head was this mother's voice.

'Peter forgot to lock the bathroom. Had no idea why he'd been locking himself in? Now I know. Oh the bruises! The scars! My hug hurt him. He pushed me away, sent me outside. He was hysterical, so I left. He wouldn't talk at all. He let me tuck him in with cocoa. All night, he tossed and turned, talked in sleep,

screamed and cried. Norman-something was mentioned, then more tears, screams, shivering...

The babysitter's just arrived. Time for my night shift.'

The lump in my throat was stuck in there and wouldn't budge.

'He made excuses – fell down, he said. Norman is 15, he said. Rough and tough. Nothing to worry about, he said. I skipped work to visit school again, talk to counsellor and teachers. All were surprised. Yes, they know Norman; they would look into it. No, I couldn't get his parents' address. Peter came home with a busted lip. Locked himself in the bathroom again. I shouted, I begged. My boss called, laid me off. Only the night job left now, cleaning public toilets. Who cares! I called some people, even John's friends, and found out where Norman lived.'

'Oh good, she's going to talk to the mum,' I thought.

'No mum around. Norman's dad was home. Drunk, high and armed. I had never been so afraid in my life. I twisted my leg falling down their stairs, trying to escape. Went to the police. Nothing they could do. I couldn't file charges – no damage done. But they would look into it, they said. I asked friends to help. Nobody would. 'Just tell Peter to stay away.' Friends turned out to be acquaintances. Back to school. Teachers annoyed, warning

me to stay away from Norman for my own good, not complicate things. I walked Peter home that day. In silence.'

This was all beginning to sound familiar. A nasty bug started gnawing inside me. My son had gotten quiet, too. This was not typical for him. I dismissed it as preteen mood swings, but deep down, I felt there was more. It was easier to ignore it. Easier, not better. Today's entry next.

'I am desperate. Need work to get food. Need to make Peter happy. Did the worst possible thing yesterday, after night shift. Got drunk. Peter left for school by himself, leaving a note. 'I'll be fine. Went to school.' Some mother I am! Showered, dressed, called teacher – she refused to talk to me. Busy, she said. Had such a nasty premonition! The manic face of Norman's dad haunted me. Cleaned Peter's room to calm myself down. Notebooks ripped, filled with threats. I couldn't believe the words I was seeing. Found Peter's trousers shoved under the bed. They smelled of urine, fresh blood stains around the zipper. I called the police – someone will look into it. Time to end this, I thought. '

I was choking on my own tears. Next passage, same date, last entry.

'I am sitting by the river, thinking about everything. I was never a scholar. No ambition, just looking to get married. Did so, had a baby, husband died. Two jobs, low pay, no prospects, but

had my son. My jewel! The only thing I did right in life! And now this! No friends, no connections, no money, my fault… I can't help him. He'd be better off without me. Some family would adopt him, live the way he deserved, good school, away from Norman. Yes, better off without me…'

I dropped the diary and jumped up. I stopped breathing altogether. My eyes scanned the water, thinking the worst. There was nobody around.

Then I saw two boys passing under the bridge in my direction. The bigger one pulled the scrawny one by the rucksack, dishing insults he had obviously picked up from an adult, without comprehending their full meaning. The smaller boy tried to run away, but couldn't. I rocketed towards them, to give Norman a piece of my mind and save Peter. Then I froze.

A woman's silhouette appeared, fragile, skinny, and plain, her back turned towards me. She stopped in front of them and said nothing. They stopped too. Peter hid tears and shame in his jacket, falling to the ground. Norman stood, ready for a fight, spite masking shock and fear. Being caught in the act was no fun. I stood still, ready to jump in at any time. The lady said nothing. She unclenched her fists and turned her face from Peter to Norman. She spread her arms wide and hugged Norman. Her son's bully winced but she still hugged him. An awkward, firm hug. She wouldn't let go, and Norman just stood there, confused. She whispered something into his ear, and his shoulders and arms relaxed. He hugged her back and tears washed down his face. She let one hand reach her son's head and gently stroked his hair. Peter rose and stood up straight. Norman fell down to his knees, crying. She leaned and hugged both boys, and the three silhouettes blended into one.

My mobile alarm vibrated and the city noise broke the moment, but only for me. The silhouette under the bridge remained still. I dropped the diary back onto the stone and hurried to catch the bus, go home, and hug my son. And talk to him, really talk. And hear.

*****

ABOUT THE AUTHOR

ANITA KOVACEVIC *is a multi-genre author and ESL (English Second Language) teacher. Despite being inordinately busy, Anita has published and illustrated an urban-legend novella (****The Threshold****) and three children's books (****Winky's Colours****,* ***The Good Pirate*** *and* ***Mimi Finds Her Magic****). Anita's stories and poems appear in* ***Inner Giant****, and recently* ***Awethology Light*** *and* ***December Awethology Light****. She is an avid reader, storyteller and poet, and dabbles as a songwriter and editor.*

Creativity feeds her soul, so there are always several teaching and writing projects that keep her on the go. She lives with her husband and children in Croatia and doesn't know the meaning of 'free time'.

www.AnitasHaven/Wordpress.com

OLD HABITS

Elizabeth Horton-Newton

Gaunt Thibideaux was a man of habits. Some people in the town of Burkesville said he was set in his ways. That's the way folks talked in Burkesville. In the summer Gaunt would mow his yard three times a week, Monday, Wednesday and Saturday, whether it needed it or not. If it rained, as it frequently did in summer in Burkesville, Gaunt would wait for a break and mow between showers. In the fall he raked his leaves on the same schedule. In the winter if it snowed, which it rarely did in Burkesville, he would shovel on the same schedule.

Every morning in fall, winter, and spring Gaunt would drive to work along the same route. Down Hickory, the street on which his eighty-seven-year-old semi-Victorian sat, left onto Pine and past the school bus stop, then onto Old Woodmill Road until he came to Route 117. However, in summer he would change slightly and take Hickory to High School Road, where the town's only high school sat, along with the community pool and park where families would gather in the summer to splash and play and generally relax in the hot Burkesville sun.

Gaunt Thibideaux was a creature of habit, because Gaunt had a secret. Gaunt enjoyed watching the children. He mostly liked the younger ones. Something about their innocence touched his heart. He would watch them on the first day of school every fall, gathered at the school bus stop looking slightly anxious in their shiny new shoes. The boys would group together sometimes punching one another lightly on the arms in an effort to overcome the uneasiness they felt at the prospect of facing new teachers and new lessons. The girls would stand in small clusters, whispering among themselves, casting glances at the boys and making unkind comments about the other girls and their new school clothes. He would slow his truck as he passed, always careful in case some impatient youngster ran across the road, eager to greet a friend. This also allowed him the opportunity to scan the groups of children and observe them in the scientific manner of a researcher noting the habits of strange yet somehow familiar creatures.

Fall was his favorite time of year. It was the time when the children were most vulnerable, when their uncertainty throbbed with a visceral energy. In winter they would be bundled against the cold; thick coats, wool hats pulled low over eyes, scarves wrapped securely around throats, protected from chill winds and observing eyes. In spring they were filled with energy, ready for the school year to end and the freedom of summer to begin. No longer unsure of the rules of their teachers and bonded now with their school mates, they were fearless.

+

Gaunt lay quietly in his small bed and struggled to stay awake. Each time he would begin to doze his eyes would pop open. Eventually he fell into a deep sleep as any nine-year-old who went to school and played hard would. He woke in the morning to the covers being pulled from his body and the sheet ripped from beneath him, rolling him off the wet mattress and onto the cold wood floor. She stood over his bed, hair flying around her face. "Pissy, pissy baby." She flung the wet sheet at him and the strong odor of his own urine hit him in the face.

"Day's wasting Gaunt Thibideaux. Better get up and wash off or you'll be late for school. Get these pissy bed clothes in the washer before you go." She always said "washer" with an added "r" making the word into "warsher," sounding like the name of some monster that chewed the stench from his messy sheets before spitting them back all cleaned and ready for another soaking. Gaunt wet the bed on and off until he was almost thirteen years old. He was doing his own laundry by the time he was ten. In the fall he would return home from school to see his Superman bed clothes hanging on the line. After a couple of years Superman's bright red cape had lightened to an almost pink color, and he had finally taken a pair of sewing shears to the sheets.

His thin mattress had been flipped from one side to the other until both sides had uneven stains that ran dark brown around the edges. He didn't get a new mattress until he went to live with his aunt and uncle. Aunt Sadie also got him a waterproof mattress pad. Unlike the thin mattress of his childhood, the mattress pad caused his urine to pool around him and he would wake in the middle of the night. Gaunt would quietly remove the wet bed clothes and start them washing before returning to his small bedroom and curling up on the thin rug that lay beside his bed, his coverlet wound around him like a death shroud.

Aunt Sadie and Uncle Bud never discussed his night time problem. He did overhear them one time ascribing it to the horror of finding his mother and stepfather sliced and diced. It may have been their kindness that got him past that humiliating part of his life. By the time he was thirteen the bed wetting had stopped entirely. He continued to do his own laundry. He didn't want Aunt Sadie to discover the other new type of stains that had become part of his nightly routine.

Gaunt's first vehicle was his late stepfather's old red pick-up. It sat in his Uncle Bud's back yard. It sat there from the day Gaunt went to live with Uncle Bud after the misfortune that took his mother and stepfather. Gaunt was twelve when it happened. He came home from church to find his mother laying in a pool of drying blood on the kitchen floor, flies buzzing merrily around her dead body. The hot August sun shone through the open kitchen window and the hole in the screen where the flies gathered in a hungry frenzy.

Amazingly, Gaunt kept his cool and called the police. Long before the recording of 911 calls, the police dispatcher recalled the call clearly. It was the biggest crime in Burkesville in fifteen years.

"This is Gaunt Thibideaux. I just came home from church and my mother is dead on the floor."

Jessie Lee Bowen inhaled sharply. "Gaunt? Gaunt Thibideaux? Are you sure she's dead? Did you try to wake her up?"

"No ma'am. I didn't try to wake her."

"Well Gaunt maybe she's just passed out from heat. Can you try to wake her?" Jessie Lee was already signaling Deputy Floyd, who sat tilted back in the Chief's office chair sucking an icy Coke from a glass bottle.

"Ma'am, there's blood everywhere. I'm pretty sure she's dead." Gaunt's voice remained steady as though he was discussing finding a dead and bloody mouse.

The mention of blood got Jessie Lee's attention and she began to gesture at the deputy more frantically. "Well Gaunt, can you tell where the blood is coming from?"

"Everywhere." Gaunt said it simply.

Wordlessly, Jessie Lee handed the phone to the deputy. Her mouth hung open, the beads of sweat on her upper lip creating a translucent moustache.

"Gaunt, this is Dep'ty Floyd, son. What's going on there?" Deputy Floyd hooked his thumb in a belt loop, thrusting his hips slightly forward.

"Hello Deputy Floyd. I just came home from church and my mother is dead," Gaunt began again.

Deputy Floyd and Jessie Lee stared at one another as Gaunt repeated his cool and dispassionate revelation. "Son, is anyone else in the house?" Deputy Floyd struggled to pull his gun belt off the back of the chair where he had so recently reclined, knocking the glass Coke bottle to the floor in the process. Jessie Lee never moved but continued staring at the deputy as though entranced by his ungainly acrobatics. Holding the phone between his chin and his shoulder, the deputy put on his belt. "Now Gaunt I want you to listen to me boy. I want you to get outside the house as quick and quiet as you can. You hear me boy?"

"Yes sir. Get out quick and quiet." Gaunt swatted at a fly that landed on his hand that was resting comfortably on the table.

"We're on our way. Now go on son." Without waiting for a response Deputy Floyd dropped the phone into its cradle and headed for the door, calling back over his shoulder, "Jessie Lee, get on the horn and get the Chief and see if you can get Doc Martin on the phone."

Jessie Lee was about to point out there didn't seem to be much need for the doctor but the deputy was already out the door. It took him less than five minutes to pull up in front of the Thibideaux residence and he was relieved to see Gaunt outside, although he was not too pleased to see him sitting on the front porch swing.

"Get off there boy and go stand by my car," he hissed, gesturing somewhat frantically at Gaunt.

Obligingly, Gaunt got up from the swing and moved down the front steps, passing within a few inches of the deputy, who had drawn his service revolver. Floyd glanced at the boy quickly and noted he was in shock, his eyes staring straight ahead and his movements almost robotic.

As soon as the deputy moved into the house the coppery scent of blood assailed him. One hand went up to cover his nose and mouth as he followed the odor into the kitchen. Gaunt's report had not prepared him for the mess that lay on the kitchen floor. Slapping his hand over his mouth, he stumbled back out the front door and ended up vomiting over the side of the front porch, knocking several wine cooler bottles into the dirt. As he wiped his handkerchief across his mouth he looked up to see Gaunt standing beside the patrol car, arms hanging loosely at his sides. A chill touched the back of his neck and he shivered slightly. For a brief moment a warning light went off in his head but he shrugged it away. He put Gaunt's odd behavior off as shock. After all, what twelve-year-old boy wouldn't be horrified to find his mother stabbed to death on the kitchen floor?

+

Gaunt had never known his biological father. He knew what he looked like from the pictures in the old album his mother kept on the top shelf of her bedroom closet along with an assortment of strange items he could not identify until he was an adult. He knew some things about the man from those evenings when his mother became inexplicably depressed and would sit on the front porch drinking wine coolers with exotic names and colors like red Bahama Mama, blue Hurricane, and bright yellow Hard Lemonade. He'd tasted the remains of a Hard Lemonade once and spit it out quickly. It didn't taste anything like the sweet/sour drink he enjoyed on hot summer days. On those occasions when Mama would start lining up empty bottles on the porch rail she would speak vividly of his father. "You look just like him," she'd say in a wistful tone. She talked about what she called silly music, poetry, rabbits with French names, and something called a Prairie Home Companion. Sometimes she would sing songs like "Dead Puppies," "Dead Skunk in the Middle of the Road," or "Nature Trail to Hell." The morning after one of these episodes she would religiously clean off the porch, ask if she had been particularly loud, and warn Gaunt earnestly about the dangers of alcohol and how he should never drink because he was born to like it too much. It was the one piece of advice she gave that he took and stood by. Except for that one swallow of Hard Lemonade, he never touched alcohol.

Even after his stepfather came along and Mama and Big Walter would drink and dance around the house a couple of Saturdays a month he never felt the urge to drink. Part of him didn't care for the taste but a larger, wiser part knew that alcohol could loosen the tongue and what was it his Mama used to say, loose lips sank ships. He had no interest in sinking any ships, especially any he happened to be sailing through life on.

Gaunt's only other passion (that neighbors knew about) was gardening. Something about digging in the cool moist soil on a fresh spring morning made him feel peaceful. He would be standing at the window that overlooked the garden out back and the sky would turn a certain shade of blue: cerulean. Gaunt loved the word cerulean. He had learned it the year his mother died, when a guidance counselor at school advised he begin keeping a journal of his feelings. The counselor, well-meaning but never understanding, had tritely stated that writing down his feelings might better help him when he felt "blue." He had restrained the giggle that threatened to bubble from his tightly compressed lips and nodded wordlessly, looking down at his hands in his lap. Determined to find a more accurate word to describe this "blue" feeling he was supposed to deal with, he had read dictionaries, poems, and short stories before stumbling across cerulean. And it was then he recognized that cerulean was the color of his eyes, the color of the sky the day his mother and stepfather were buried, and the bright free blue he felt when he emerged from the shell he had been encased in for years. It was the color of the sky the day Cindy's blood had run into the sparkling creek, the color of the dress his mother wore when the knife split the fabric and blooms of red rose across the front like spring's blossoms.

+

Cindy Hensley may have been the first one. It may have been deliberate or the result of an accident, games played too roughly, violence gone too far. Whatever the reason, Cindy was the one accepted as the first one. Cindy was petite, dark hair often worn in short ponytails, skin pale and almost translucent. Cindy was fifteen but looked barely more than twelve. Ostracized by most of her sophomore class because she was considered "strange," "unfriendly," or just because she was different, Cindy usually walked to and from school and usually did it alone. Perhaps this made her an easy first target. Perhaps she wanted to be a target. Being an outcast could be a lonely and painful existence.

Gaunt had seen the other kids teasing her. He'd watched her lower lip tremble and her eyes fill with tears when she walked past Barrett's Drugstore, where most kids gathered after school or on Saturday afternoons. He'd heard the laughter and the comments about her clothes when she came to church with her step-father. The man always walked with his hand at the small of her back and something about it made Gaunt feel strangely excited. It was almost as if the man was her boyfriend escorting her to a school dance instead of a parent taking her to church. Cindy's mother no longer attended church. She'd had a bad accident several years earlier shortly after marrying Cindy's stepfather, and was confined to a wheelchair. "Pity," Gaunt thought, "She was kind of pretty for someone's mother." Cindy had inherited her mother's previous good looks and Gaunt thought she might someday be kind of pretty too.

Cindy walked with her eyes downcast, avoiding the catcalls and comments from the school crowd. Gaunt was sweeping the sidewalk in front of the drug store, casting surreptitious glances at the posturing boys and flirty girls who gathered on the corner. Gaunt watched Ashley and Heather, known as the Grimley sisters, break off from the group and start to follow Cindy. Although he couldn't hear what they were saying it was apparent Cindy could for she began to walk more quickly. As he turned to take the broom back inside the store he heard Billy Ray comment, "They said she smelled like piss at gym class today and Ashley said her granny panties had a yellow stain in the crotch. Pissy pants."

The crowd giggled and muttered pissy pants repeatedly. Gaunt made no comment and after placing the broom in the back room he said good afternoon to Mr. Barrett and grabbed his books from the shelf under the counter.

"You want to grab a cold one," Barrett joked as he always did when Gaunt was leaving.

And, as he always did, Gaunt replied, "I appreciate it Mr. Barrett." He took a cold bottle of Coke from the cooler, icy water dripping into the melting cubes, and popped the top off using the opener that hung on a string beside the cooler. "Thanks again Mr. Barrett."

"Have a good one son," Barrett called as he turned to make a milk shake for Veronica and Stevie, the most popular couple at school.

Gaunt stood on the sidewalk for a few seconds watching the retreating backs of the school crowd as they headed to their homes, or to ball practice. Then he looked in the direction Cindy and her tormentors had taken. They were crossing Main and heading down to the bridge that crossed into Morning Glory Woods, aptly named for the woods that grew on both sides of the bridge. Beneath the bridge a thin trickle of a creek struggled over small stones. When the weather cooled it would become a shiny streak of ice. Gaunt saw Cindy hesitate a moment then watched as the Grimley sisters threw back their heads, obviously laughing at some joke. Suddenly Cindy bolted and ran down the small path that led to the creek. Ashley and Heather turned and headed back in Gaunt's direction. Tipping the bottle, Gaunt let the cool sweet liquid run down his throat. Then he started the walk home. As he passed the Grimley sisters Ashley called out, "Be careful on the bridge, Gaunt Thibideaux. Something smells mighty bad over there." This reduced the girls to hysterical laughter and they dashed down the street as though they had told the funniest joke in the world.

Gaunt continued on his way. As he started across the bridge he glanced back over his shoulder. Main Street was empty. It was that quiet space of time when mothers were home starting supper, daddies were still at work, and kids were either engaged in homework or the practice of a seasonal sport. Quietly, Gaunt moved down the skinny path to the creek. He didn't see her right away. And she neither saw nor heard his approach. She was leaning against an old beech tree and something about the way she was standing looked odd. Gaunt realized she was standing with her legs squeezed tightly together as though she was holding something between them. He heard a muffled sniffle and then the odor of fresh urine hit him.

Something hot turned in the pit of Gaunt's stomach, something hot and heavy and dark. "Hey," he called softly.

Cindy gasped and spun to face him.

He proffered the Coke bottle. "Want some Coke?"

Cindy shook her head. "Go away."

"It's okay. I know how you feel." He took two more steps toward her bringing him close enough to reach out and touch her if he wanted to.

Cindy tried to move away and a dark stain spread across the front of her capris. Her face grew red and she crossed her legs as though the action might hide her sin.

Gaunt watched the stain spread and a pounding began in his head. "Why do you let them do that to you?" His voice was soft and curious.

Cindy did not respond but fat tears began to well up in her eyes (her strange sky blue eyes, Gaunt thought from a distance) and then they streaked down her face. A bubble of snot appeared in one nostril. She looked for all the world like some stupid animal brought to the slaughter. Her eyes widened in surprise as the bottle slammed into the side of her head. She stood staring at Gaunt, eyes wide and mouth opened in a silent "oh."

The bottle came back across the other side of her head and broke, the slivers of glass looking like a cloud of crystals in the speckled sunlight that danced through the leaves.

"Why?" Gaunt asked again as Cindy staggered and leaned heavily against the tree trunk before sliding jerkily to the ground.

Gaunt moved closer and squatted before her. She stared at him her breathing coming in small gasps. Her mouth opened and closed but no sound came out. The broken bottle slid across her the vein that throbbed in her throat and the blood burst out in the sun like rubies. Spatters flew across his face, warm and salty on his lips. "Why?" he asked one last time as release came and he felt the hot flood of completion. He watched as her breathing slowed then stopped. Gingerly he felt for a heartbeat like they did on the doctor shows his mother had liked to watch in the afternoon. There was a little pulsing, like the vibrations when a car passed in the distance, and then there was nothing.

Gaunt stood up and looked down at the bright red drops of blood that speckled his shirt. "Now that's gonna be a problem," said a strange voice from somewhere behind and above him. He glanced up to see the older man looking down at the mess Cindy created at the base of the tree. "We need to figger this out quick son."

It only took Gaunt a moment to recognize his father. The red plaid flannel shirt, the glasses a tad too big for his narrow face, the baggy jeans that hung low on his slim hips, and most peculiar of all, the facial resemblance.

"I didn't mean to, Daddy." He had never used the word out loud before and it felt strange rolling off his tongue.

"Well, that's neither here nor there," Daddy said matter-of-factly, "It is what it is and we need to get this mess straightened out." Daddy rubbed the fine blond stubble on his chin. "First off I'd take the rest of that bottle down to the creek and smash it real good on the rocks so no fingerprints can be found." Scratching his cowlick he continued, "Then take off that shirt and start heading home. Stay in the woods till you reach Cotter's field then cut through his corn until you get to the road. When you're sure there's nothing coming down the road take off to the other side. It's less than a quarter of a mile to your backyard. I'll think about the rest while you get going."

Gaunt immediately set to obeying his father's instructions. He only improvised slightly by walking in the creek and washing the blood off his leather tennis shoes and leaving no trail of footprints from the Cindy mess. It was still blazing hot and no one would think anything of a young boy walking in the cool creek without a shirt if anyone saw him. As he cut through the corn he heard his Daddy breathing hard beside him. "Okay here's what you need to do." The next set of instructions came quick and soft, interrupted by an occasional deep breath, as they ran through the corn. "You gotta burn the shirt."

Gaunt slowed as he digested the suggestion. "Where?" Silence met the question and he could hear the sound of a lawnmower not far off. It was probably coming from home. Uncle Bud had asked him to mow the sparse patch of grass he called the front yard. He should have been home earlier. Uncle Bud would figure out he was late because … Gaunt stopped suddenly. The sound of the lawnmower had ceased and he could hear his uncle swearing loudly. The old machine locked up every so often and Gaunt was the only one who could get it started. The screen door slammed in the distance as Uncle Bud's voice faded. The lawn mower had blades, blades Gaunt had sharpened earlier in the week in preparation for the mowing.

Moving quickly and stealthily through the corn Gaunt emerged in the yard. The lawnmower sat silent and stalled.

"Don't do it boy!" His father cautioned. "You could lose a finger or even a hand messin' with that old grass cutter."

"Shut up old man!" Gaunt hissed and moved to the lawnmower, kneeling beside it. Keeping his eyes on the screen door he put on his blood speckled shirt and took a deep breath. He rolled the machine onto its side and looked at the grass clogged blades and the piece of rock wedged between them. The blades glittered invitingly in spite of the coating of green. He waited a few seconds to hear if his father would protest again but the only sounds were the breeze crackling through the corn, the sound of the TV from inside the house, and the chirping of insects and birds. Gaunt watched his own hand reach down to the rock and just before his long fingers touched it he closed his eyes. The rock flew free and the blades whipped into action and Gaunt heard the scream before he realized it was coming from his own mouth.

Something warm and wet hit his face and the screen door slammed and Uncle Bud was screaming too as he ran across the scrappy old yard. The screen door slammed again and his Aunt Sadie's scream joined the cacophony of screams and birdcalls as a flock of crows rose in a dark cloud momentarily casting a shadow across the liquid garnet of his hand.

"Christ on a cross!" Uncle Bud swore as he ripped off his sweaty yellowed tee shirt and wrapped it around Gaunt's hand. Gaunt stared at him blankly. Concern etched the lines on Uncle Bud's face. Then Aunt Sadie was pushing the old man aside and shouting for him to get the truck. As Bud ran off to get the truck she tied the tee shirt tightly around his hand, ignoring the speckles of blood that dotted the front of her faded yellow blouse and the reddened dust that soiled her bony knees below her cut-off shorts. Somehow Gaunt was bundled into the front seat of the truck between his aunt and uncle as they sped toward town. Sadie continually stroked his head, murmuring words that made no sense and Bud cast quick nervous glances at him. When they reached Doc Miller's, Bud pulled haphazardly into a parking spot and half carried Gaunt into the office.

It was cool and strangely quiet inside. Mary Miller, Doc's wife and secretary, stood up behind the newly installed counter that separated the waiting area from the office. "We're closed for the day…" her voice trailed off and her eyes widened behind her thick glasses when she saw the bright red tee shirt wrapped around Gaunt's hand. "Oh my stars!" she exclaimed before calling "Doctor!" and hurrying down the hall toward the exam rooms.

A flurry of activity ensued and Gaunt struggled to stay conscious. Sometimes he would see that red flannel shirt in the background and think how he was smarter than his daddy had ever been. There wasn't a lot of pain but the rich coppery scent of his blood filed his head making him retch. Mary Miller shoved a puke bowl under his chin causing his mouth to snap shut and his teeth to clack loudly.

"Jesus Mary! Be careful!" Doc muttered.

Mary's hands were shaking and she never answered. Gaunt briefly wondered if she should be holding the puke bowl under her own chin. Her eyes were popping like two dark bubbles about to burst behind her chunky lenses.

In the end, when the blood was cleared away, Gaunt had only lost the tips of one thumb and two fingers on his left hand. But his shirt was covered in blood and had to be thrown away. He watched as Mary Miller rolled it up and marveled that both his and Cindy Hensley's blood was now blended in a deep dark design forever linking them as shadowy lovers. He shivered at the thought and was stunned as Aunt Sadie's arms went around him comfortingly. "It's okay Gaunt. You're gonna be fine."

Gaunt nodded wordlessly. He was going to be fine. Cindy Hensley was going to be fine too as she lay at the foot of the old tree. No one would tease her until she wet her pants and cried ever again. Cindy was free. He had set her free.

+

Gaunt had worked at Claudie's Diner since his junior year in high school. It was his first job. It was his only real job. In middle school he'd helped around Barrett's Fountain and Drugs for change and pops. But his job at Claudie's was his first real weekly paycheck job. He had started working after school until close, washing dishes, bussing tables, cleaning up. Then old Frank, Claudie's live-in, started teaching him grilling. Grilling was more of a skill than most people realized. It required knowing exactly how long it took to go from raw to rare to medium, to well, and all the stages in between. Scrambled eggs soft were nothing like the more rubbery scrambled eggs well. Gaunt paid close attention and when Frank had the stroke that left his left arm paralyzed into a hook and his legs as rubbery as well-cooked eggs, Gaunt stepped into the role of grill cook effortlessly. When he graduated high school he blew off the chance to go to college and took on full-time hours at Claudie's. There were those who believed he was afraid of leaving home. But most were glad he chose to remain in Burkesville, where he was known as the best grill cook in a "hunnert" miles.

Gaunt enjoyed grilling. Gaunt enjoyed everything about his job at Claudie's. Grilling and all the side labor kept part of his mind busy while freeing the other part, the secret part, to explore darker work. Gaunt worked every day, switching off with whoever Claudie hired to fill in part-time. No one stayed in the job long. High schoolers would work long enough to earn the money to buy a car or prom tickets, drifters worked long enough to earn enough money to move on to greener pastures, and sometimes single mothers would take up working at the diner to buy Christmas for their kids. But Gaunt and Claudie were the only permanent fixtures at the diner. Except for Frank, who would sit in his wheelchair by the side window, staring blankly out at the Gas-N-Go, watching truckers fill up their rigs and kids on bikes run in and out with ice creams and soda pops. Every hour or so, Gaunt would replace the cup of coffee by his right hand, whether

Frank had drunk from it or not. He'd pat Frank on the shoulder and set down the cup, neither saying a word.

Gaunt wasn't one to venture far from home. He couldn't say what drew him to the State Fair almost two hundred miles from home. Maybe it was the ad in the daily paper. Maybe it was the radio commercials advertising games, prizes, circus acts, and more! Most likely it was the poster the young girl in the gypsy costume asked to place in the window of Claudie's. Claudie was home sick that day and Frank was home with her.

The short, slender, dark haired girl in the colorful attire came into the diner, chains and bangles jangling and flashing in the strong fall sunlight. It was pretty clear she was young even though she wore heavy make-up in an effort to appear older.

She leaned on the counter, her small breasts straining against the corset-type bodice of her short flouncy dress. The bright purples and peacock blues, the black mesh stockings and the over the knee faux black leather boots made her look like a wayward trick-or-treater out a month early.

"Hey meester," she called across the counter, assuming an unidentifiable accent. "The fair is coming. We be there. Me and my family we tell fortunes, have lucky tokens, take off curses. You come see us?" Her bow mouth turned up at the corners. It might have been appealing except her lipstick was a dark red and caked on her lips, smearing slightly outside her lip line as if to make her lips appear fuller and more sensuous.

She held up the poster. "See here, meester. Can I put this in your window? Tell everybody come see the shows." Then pouting slightly, she added, "You let me put sign I tell your fortune right now, no charge."

Gaunt stared at her in fascination. Her dark hair was covered by a colorful scarf, but stray strands escaped and clung to her forehead. "You can tell my future?"

"Sure can. Me gran-mama come from the old country. We special people. Have special gifts. You show me palm, I tell you future."

Gaunt laid his hand on the counter never taking his eyes from the strange woman child. She took his hand in her tiny one and ran her fingers lightly over his palm. "Ah. I see much here. Very much. You lucky man." Looking up at him from below her long and obviously false eyelashes, she ran her tongue over her lips. "Usually I charge for reading. But you are so kind to let me put sign in window so I give you a taste of what I offer. You come to fair and see me, I give you big discount."

Gaunt watched her mouth as she spoke. She had a slight overbite and her two front teeth were a little crooked. "Okay."

Her smile widened and she bent forward, causing her breasts to press up almost escaping the confines of her bodice. Her warm, moist breath blew across his palm and she ran her fingertip lightly along the lines that scored his skin. "You have very long life line, very long. And I see good fortune soon in your future." Then, a small frown creased her forehead. She gazed up at him sorrowfully. "Oh but you have had broken heart. Mean girl hurt you." She went back to his palm, drawing his hand closer to her body, his fingertips almost touching her breast.

Brightening, she tilted her head. "Ah, but I see new love coming to you. Very soon she will come. Maybe, maybe even already here. Very special love. She come from far away to find you." Licking her lips again. "But you come see me at fair and I be able to tell you more."

Gaunt studied her eyes. "I will definitely see you at the fair. Do you have flyers as well as your sign? I'd be happy to hand them out for you. I'm sure a lot of people would like to know their futures."

"Hmm, no. Maybe I can get some and come back to see you before the fair." Her accent slipped for a moment and a thrill went through Gaunt.

"Okay. Go ahead and put your sign up." He drew his hand slowly from hers, allowing his fingertips to graze her palm as he did. "What's your name so I know who to ask for when I go to the fair?"

A shadow seemed to cross her face and her eyes grew hooded. He wondered if she sensed something and he quickly straightened. "Of course I do work a lot. I hope I get there."

This seemed to clear any concerns she had. "I am Zina. You must come. I see so much to tell you. And I give you very big discount for your kindness."

Gaunt nodded. She was caught like a bug in amber. "I'll make sure to be there."

Offering a smile, she turned and, skirt flouncing, went to the window to tape up her sign. As she left the diner she cast one final look at Gaunt and waved with her fingers like a little girl saying "bye-bye" to a favorite uncle.

Old Bill had been sitting at the counter watching the whole exchange. "Gaunt Thibideaux, don't you go spending all your money on that one. She's a huckster. You can't trust carney folk."

A wide grin split Gaunt's face. "Oh, I know, Bill. I'm not going to the fair. I was just having a little fun."

Bill laughed and shook his head. "I always say you're a smart one, too smart for Burkesville."

With that, Gaunt went back to the grill humming softly as he began to clean up. It took him a few minutes to realize he was humming a tune his mother used to sing to him at bedtime—"Dream A Little Dream of Me." Gaunt chuckled.

A few hours later as he turned out the lights and closed the window shades he pulled the poster from the window. It would be better not to have the fair advertised in his window.

That Sunday, Claudie closed the diner early. Traffic was slow and she opined a lot of folks had gone to the fair.

"Why don't you go on over there and have a little fun, Gaunt? A young man needs to play sometimes." She winked conspiratorially.

Gaunt cocked his head to one side as if contemplating the suggestion. The memory of the small gypsy girl with tiny hands filled his mind. Shaking his head, Gaunt responded. "No thanks Claudie. It's going to be crowded and noisy, two things I don't care for. I think I'll head on home and watch a little television, maybe rent a video."

Shaking her head, Claudie followed Gaunt to the back door, holding it open as he ducked outside. "You need to get out Gaunt. You ain't gonna find a wife in your living room."

Gaunt chuckled; a strange gurgling sound that began deep in his chest and erupted more like a donkey braying than a human laugh. "I'm not looking for a wife, Claudie. I'm fine just the way I am."

Gaunt did not like being in crowds, surrounded by people who pushed and shoved, bumping into him without apology. Parking his truck at the far end of the parking lot adjacent to the fairgrounds, he made his way slowly to the ticket booth. The scent of frying food, farm animals, and the cloying odors of crowds of people pressing past one another assailed his nostrils. Gaunt glanced at the map that had been provided with the price of his admission.

Moving through the crowds, avoiding contact as much as possible, he made his way past concession stands, games of chance, and hawkers enticing the passers-by to play. He walked past the fortune teller tent as an older woman called out to a group of teen girls to come find out who they would marry. The girls giggled, pushing one another to go in and have a palm read. They annoyed him with their gullibility, the ease with which they could be seduced by a smooth talker to part with their money and their dignity.

Stopping at a food stand he purchased a cold drink and wound his way back to a bench from which he could observe the comings and goings of fortune seeking fools. Soon the old woman was replaced, and Gaunt's eyes narrowed as Zina called out to a group of young boys, flashing her smile and touching one boy's arm possessively. Even as his friends continued one boy remained, head cocked to one side, as he listened to what Zina was telling him. Gaunt watched as she took the boy's hand into her tiny hand and ran her finger across his palm in a familiar movement. She tilted her head, smiling seductively, stepping toward the entrance to tent and gently tugging on the boy's hand. He looked helplessly after his friends, who disappeared into the throngs, oblivious to his discomfort.

Gaunt watched as Zina and her prey disappeared into the tent and the older woman stepped outside. She was soon joined by a middle aged man dressed colorfully in what might be considered gypsy attire. They spoke briefly and then they laughed. The man shook his head, an expression of distaste on his face. Time seemed to pass slowly as Gaunt waited. Finally, Zina and her customer emerged from the tent, the boy's face flushed. Zina said a few words to the gypsy man before taking the boy's arm, pulling him close to her and guiding him toward the parking lot. Tossing his empty drink cup into an overflowing trash can, Gaunt followed discreetly behind them.

The sun had set and the bright lights of the fair cast strange shadows on the faces of revellers. As Gaunt strode purposefully past them he blinked hard to clear the vision of cadaverous faces and sometimes smiling skulls that assaulted him. The odors of sweat and decay caused him to almost gag. Focusing on Zina's colorful costume he pushed all thoughts from his mind. She led the boy through a gate at the back of the park with a large handwritten sign that read "Employees and Vendors Only."

Debating only a moment, he looked quickly around before moving quickly through the gate. He thought he had lost them when the sound of a giggle and the jangle of her bracelets caught his attention. He rounded a corner in time to see them dart into a camper.

Moving to stand beneath the shadow of the trees that bordered the parking lot and the fairgrounds he murmured, "As Moliere said, 'the best reply to unseemly behavior is patience and moderation.'"

Leaning against the thick trunk of an old oak he watched as a dim light went on inside the camper. A few cicadas still chirped as the fall had not completely set in. Occasionally a small animal would rustle through the leaves and grass. Gaunt would move his foot slightly and it would scurry away. Time seemed to pass slowly like the moments spent waiting for the medication to kick in and the headache to pass; craving the second when the agony would end and blessed relief would come. He struggled to keep his breathing regular and heartbeat steady.

It was only fifteen short minutes before the camper door opened and the young man stepped out. Zina followed him, tossing her hair back over her shoulders, her scarf no longer confining those dark locks. Gaunt watched as they returned to the employee entrance and when the gate closed behind them he moved quickly and quietly to follow. They parted with no sign of affection, Zina returning to the tent and the young man heading along the midway. He pulled a cell phone from his pocket and head turning from side to side as he searched for someone, he made a call. Stopping dead, his voice raised but his words not clear, he stopped looking around. Evidently whatever he sought in the crowd was not going to appear. Shoving the phone into the pocket of his jeans he hurried toward the parking lot.

Gaunt watched him go. He glanced back toward the tent. A sweet smile touched his lips and for a moment he looked like a teenager again. Zina was talking to the gypsy man and laughing as she handed him what appeared to be a wallet. His decision made, he headed purposefully toward the parking lot.

The young man stood beside a late model sports car and dug in his pants pocket, obviously searching for his keys. Suddenly he stopped and began patting his pockets. “Damn it!” He swore loudly and slammed his hand on the roof of the car. Gaunt approached him cautiously.

"Excuse me young man?"

Head turning sharply, eyes narrowed angrily, the boy responded, "What?"

"I'm plain clothes security here at the fair and I wondered if I could ask you a few questions." He kept his voice soft and even.

The boy looked nervously at his car then back at Gaunt. "Yeah sure. Is there a problem?"

Gaunt moved closer, keeping his eyes locked on the boy's. "Would you mind checking to be sure you have your wallet, sir?"

Eyes widening, the boy patted his pants pockets as though he had not already realized he'd been ripped off by the gypsy girl. "It's gone! Someone must have picked my pocket."

Now Gaunt was only a step away, and even though he spoke softly the boy could hear him easily. "It's okay son. This doesn't have to go any further. I observed you with the gypsy girl and I believe she lifted your property. I will be happy to escort you back to the scene and we can confront her and get your wallet back. I saw her returning to the camper after you parted.

"If you'll follow me we can go in the back way and avoid any embarrassment."

The boy nodded. "Will she be arrested?"

Gaunt began walking and the boy fell into step beside him. "If you choose to press charges; that can be done. Now that would create a bit of a stir and of course we'd be looking at a trial. I'd be happy to lock them all up but most of the guys prefer not to raise a ruckus. You know considering the situation ..." Gaunt left the sentence hanging, the implication clear.

They had reached the edge of the woods that circled behind the employee parking area. Trees still thick with leaves in spite of the carpet that had begun to fall surrounded them. "Yeah maybe if we can just get my wallet back…"

"I understand. It's embarrassing. Did she ask you for money?" Gaunt angled so the boy was slightly ahead of him now.

Clearing his throat uncomfortably the boy nodded, glancing back over his shoulder. "After…"

"I have to admit I don't get it. You seem like a nice kid; attractive and smart. Why would you even want to hit that?"

The boy stopped short and turned to face him. "I-I don't know. She was just so persuasive." He was sweating slightly and even in the darkness Gaunt could see tears forming in his eyes.

"How old are you?" Gaunt asked gently, slipping his hand into his pants pocket.

"Sixteen. My parents will kill me if they find out." His voice shook.

Gaunt reached out and patted his shoulder comfortingly. "Hey, we all make mistakes. It pissed me off when I saw them laughing at you." He glanced down at the front of the boy's pants and noted his fly was partly opened. "Zip up."

Further embarrassed, the boy reached down to zip his pants smiling gratefully at Gaunt's kindness, and the knife came up swiftly, slicing easily across the young throat, freshly shaved that morning and still smooth. A look of surprise crossed his face and his mouth opened and closed like a fish out of water. Then his hands clawed at his throat as he felt the heat of his blood begin to spread down the front of his shirt. The look of surprise had turned to one of questioning, his eyes seeming to ask "Why?"

Gaunt spun him around and tenderly lowered him to the grass and leaves. Kneeling behind him, allowing the body to lean against his he whispered in the soft ear, "Shh. It's alright now. You should never let them laugh at you. Don't let them make you cry."

The boy's body jerked as he tried to move away from Gaunt, his feet digging into the leaves, crunching them as he struggled. Soon the struggles became less and the gurgling slowed and stopped. The body rested limply against Gaunt's hard body as both men felt the release of the moment.

Bending his head back, Gaunt could see the stars through the trees and off to the west a full harvest moon hung low in the sky. The face seemed to smile kindly at him, pleased with him.

Laying the boy's body in the foliage, he rose and pulled off his own shirt. Amazingly, there was very little blood on it. The boy's face glowed in the thin moonlight, streaks of glistening black stretching down the front of his body and onto the leaves that surrounded him.

Gaunt took a deep breath and plunged the knife into the moist soil to clean the blood. Pulling the body to a sitting position, he managed to get his own shirt on over the boy's blood-soaked garment. Gaunt was strong. It took little effort for him to pull the body up and slinging the limp arm around his neck he half carried, half dragged it to the edge of the woods.

A crowd of young people were piling into a van toward the front of the parking lot, far away from where Gaunt's truck sat, its outline barely visible as the moon disappeared behind clouds. He waited until they had driven off before moving quickly to his truck. Placing the body on the tarp he had already laid out in the truck bed, he rolled it up and anchored the dark package with his landscaping tools and bricks he had purchased for a garden project. He drove back to Burkesville, watching the speed limit all the way. Gaunt felt a thrill every time a car sped past him; his heart raced when a state trooper drove by, not giving him a second glance.

Pulling in to his late uncle's place, he turned off his head lights and sat quietly in the truck for several minutes. The only sound was the clicking of the truck's engine as it cooled. Leaning his head back against the seat, he stared out at the full moon that hung lazily over the dilapidated house. No one lived there now. It stood empty, a ghost of days gone by. The old shed sat in the deeper shadows beyond the house and at its side, the truck that had offered his first freedom. It gleamed in the moonlight, a beacon calling him to join it, to once again climb into the driver's seat and ride to new adventures. Of course the motor barely worked now, struggling to turn over when the key was turned in the ignition. Yet it still served a purpose.

Gaunt stepped out of the truck and stretched, his bones and joints creaking as the tension was released from his body. After a glance around, he climbed into the bed of the truck and set about removing his secret package. The boy's body no longer held any fascination for him. The lifeless form was nothing more than a used up object to be disposed of, hidden away from prying eyes.

Climbing into the old truck, inhaling the familiar scent of mold and decay, he turned the key. The engine struggled to life, the seat beneath him trembling with anticipation. Gaunt rolled it back several feet, revealing a large wooden board that had been hidden by the vehicle. Humming under his breath, he jumped out of the truck and pulled the board aside exposing a deep hole. The moonlight barely revealed the sides of the gap in the ground. A sweet and sickly scent rose into the night air. Bending his head back so the moonlight shone on his face, Gaunt sniffed the air appreciatively. An expression of pleasure lit his visage. Eyes closed, a subtle smile on his lips, he stood a few moments, revelling in the peace that flooded his body. Then in one neat and quick moved he grabbed the corners of the tarp and rolled the boy's body into the hole. The thump of the corpse landing at the bottom seemed to split the night and Gaunt looked quickly around. Other than the soft rustling of the grass and weeds in the slight breeze, the distant scrambling of some small animal, and the occasional click of an insect, the night was still.

Gaunt pulled a small flashlight from his pants pocket and directed the beam into the pit. The boy's body had landed face up, arms spread wide, one leg tucked under his body, the other leg bent at a strange angle. Around him lay other bodies in varying stages of decay. Most of the remains were small, obviously children. Some were clothed, others were nude, and a few were reduced to bones. Gaunt started when he caught movement in one corner of the pit. A small wave of dark gray moved around, causing some of the bodies to stir slightly, almost as though they were coming to life.

Gaunt watched for a few moments, fascinated by the rats that celebrated his latest donation to their gory feast. With a sigh he replaced the board, got back into the old track and drove it back over the hole, once again concealing it from the prying daylight that would soon spread across the deserted property.

Driving through the now deserted streets of Burkesville he hummed softly. In his head he heard his mother's voice singing "Dream a Little Dream of Me." He was still humming as he stepped into the shower and let the warm water wash away the sweat and dirt of the evening's activities, cleaning away the scent of the fair and the crowds that had brushed past him on the midway.

As he settled into his bed, the bed he had brought with him when he moved from his uncle's house to his own home in town, he smiled. The comforting sound of the plastic sheet rustled beneath him. In a short time he drifted into a dreamless and satisfied sleep.

+

The years passed like clouds drifting lazily across a summer sky. Sometimes in thick, fluffy puffs that seemed to hang gently, other times in thin streaks that almost stretched endlessly. Then there were those times when the clouds were heavy and dark, threatening to shower Gaunt's life with disaster.

Strangers passed through Burkesville. Some moved on, some stayed a while. There were those that chose Burkesville as their new home and those that took root involuntarily. Some folks up and left and no one really questioned it. People kept to themselves in Burkesville. If they spoke about one another, it was in hushed voices behind closed doors.

When Frank finally passed away, all the life seemed to go out of Claudie as well. She seemed to take his place and sit at a front table, staring out the window. The old Gas-n-Go finally went and was replaced by a shiny new truck stop, gas station, convenience store. They even had a grill, where a driver could grab a burger or hot dog for a buck or two. They didn't have ice cream sodas but they did offer soft serve. It wasn't real ice cream of course but the kids liked it.

On one of those heavy clouded days, Claudie approached Gaunt, pulling herself up on one of the counter stools. Several had been mended with duct tape, a thing Frank would never have permitted. Claudie grunted and shifted around trying to get comfortable on the seat that was too small for her prodigious bottom. "How do people sit on these?" she grumbled. Gaunt offered a slight smile but said nothing. There was a thickness in the air that threatened to cut off all his oxygen and send him gasping out the door.

"Gaunt, we need to talk." With that she began to tell him how she was getting old and with Frank gone she didn't have the heart to keep the diner opened. She hemmed and hawed and danced around, the words sometimes getting tangled in her mouth. Eventually, she told Gaunt what he already knew, since he had found the papers for the sale in the old desk in the corner they jokingly called the office. Gaunt was gentle, telling Claudie he not only understood, but thought it was the best thing for her.

"I've been thinking of starting my own business," Gaunt told her brightly. "Maybe as a landscaper. People are always talking about my garden."

"You do have some *wondermus* garden," Claudie agreed, using the made up word she'd abandoned years before. "Your flowers and veggies are the finest anywhere."

Gaunt nodded and patted her hand gently. "I'll have to bring you some of my Stripy tomatoes. I know you like them."

Claudie was thrilled with the offer. She certainly did like Gaunt's tomatoes. In fact, there wasn't a thing in his garden she didn't like. From his daylilies to his cukes and 'maters, Gaunt had two green thumbs and eight green fingers to go with them.

"What will you do when you close down, Claudie?" Gaunt began cleaning off the counter and checking to see if the sugar, salt, and pepper shakers were full for the morning. One thing that hadn't slowed over the years was the daily breakfast rush.

A faraway look came over the old woman's jowly face. "I've always wanted to go out west. Not to California but the old west where there were cowboys and Indians. I was thinking I might take one of them bus tours. Heck, I might even settle out there for a minute."

Gaunt nodded. "Good for you Claudie. You should enjoy yourself. You've worked hard all these years."

"Indeed I have," she agreed.

"I am a little curious about something." Gaunt leaned back against the pie case. "How come you didn't offer me the chance to buy the diner?"

A deep red flush began across Claudie's massive breasts and worked its way up across her chins to her face. "Well Gaunt, it never occurred to me that you would want to buy it."

Gaunt raised his eyebrows wordlessly.

The red grew even deeper. "And, um, I figured you wouldn't be able to afford it."

Gaunt continued to stare at her.

"I reckon you might have got a loan." She was wiggling on the stool now, her discomfort as apparent as the sweat beading on her moustached upper lip.

"I reckon I could have. But I guess I could never match what that big company offered you. And the money will come in handy for your trip."

Claudie slid off the stool and began fiddling with the napkin holders. "Yeah, I do need the money."

"Between what they pay you and what you got from Frank's insurance, you should be set. Heck, you could even take a trip around the world." Gaunt leaned his elbows on the counter, fingers laced in front of him.

"Frank's insurance?" Claudie's voice has risen a couple of octaves.

"Yes. I was kind of hoping you would have used it to fix up the diner. But I understand. I mean, after all those years taking care of him you needed something for yourself. There had to be some reward for all that hard work." Gaunt's eyes were steady, unblinking. They hypnotized Claudie the way a snake might hypnotize a rabbit.

"I-I thought about it. B-But there were so many bills ..." her voice trailed off.

Suddenly Gaunt slapped his hands on the counter. "Well, it's all water under the bridge. You go ahead and count down the drawer and I'll finish cleaning up." He came around the counter, went to the front door, locked it, and flipped the sign to close. Then he reached out and flicked off the outside lights.

When he turned back, Claudie had circled around to the cash register and was pulling out the cash and the cash bag. He walked past her into the kitchen and stood at the grill for several minutes. Frank had been a good man. His death had been hard for Gaunt. He'd watched the man waste away. Every day he grew weaker. It got to the point where he couldn't keep any food down.

Claudie had attended to him religiously. She kept jugs of the sweet tea he loved in the refrigerator, refilling his glass frequently. Gaunt figured it out the day he poured a glass of tea for himself and Claudie had paled. As soon as he took a sip he knew something was wrong. He didn't let Claudie know. He didn't tell anyone. Instead he waited. Now the waiting was over.

+

Tessa and Tommy Barrow leaned against their car and listened as the real estate agent extolling the value of the property.

Although it hadn't been kept up since the death of the owner it offered a lot of perks.

"The property itself is flat and if you're looking for a place to keep your horses it would be very easy to rebuild the fence and extend it to make a corral. The shed and the house are actually in pretty good condition. The plumbing still works." Grinning, Debra Ryan gestured toward the old truck that stood near the shed. "I wouldn't be surprised if that truck is worth something."

Tommy moved toward the shed and Tessa followed with Debra at her side. "You can see where someone kept up both a vegetable garden and a flower garden pretty recently."

Tommy had reached the truck and finding the door unlocked, opened it. Keys hung from the ignition and Tommy climbed in.

"Be careful Tommy!" Tessa called out.

Debra laughed. "Men and their trucks."

Tessa shot her a look of annoyance. She was far from impressed with what Debra called a "bargain." The sound of the engine struggling to turn over broke the quiet. "How long ago did you say the owner died?"

"Almost a year. The county spent some time trying to find next of kin. Once it reverted to the county they put it up for sale." Glancing at the sheaf of papers she carried she continued. "It belonged to Gaunt Thibideaux."

Tessa stopped short. "The guy who used to do gardening in town?"

"I really don't know," Debra admitted. "I've only lived in Burkesville for six months."

The truck engine caught and roared into life. Tommy stuck his head out of the window, grinning from ear to ear. "How about that?"

An alarm went off in Tessa's head. "Tommy!" She began to move quickly toward the truck as Tommy began to roll back toward her.

Debra hurried along behind her, her heels sinking into the soft earth of the yard.

Suddenly Tommy stopped the truck and got out. There was a wooden board where the truck had stood. It had cracked down the middle and sagged toward an indention in the yard. Tommy pulled one side back exposing a hole in the ground. A strange sickly sweet odor rose from the earth.

Tessa's hands flew to her nose. "Oh God! What is that smell?"

"Something must have fallen in and died," Tommy held a handkerchief over his nose as he pulled the other board to the side. Stepping up to the excavation he gazed down into its depths. The bright sun lit it up all the way to the bottom. Gagging, Tommy stumbled back from the pit. "Get back Tessa!"

She should have listened. But she was a woman whose curiosity far outweighed her common sense. Staring down into the cavity she felt the bile rise in her throat. Beside her she heard a scream that seemed to echo off the very air. Debra was screeching and staggering away. No sound escaped Tessa's throat nor did she move away. Hypnotized by the scramble of bones, flesh, clothing and rats she froze in place. It was only when Tommy grabbed her arm and pulled her away that she moved.

The trio hurried toward their cars, Tommy already pulling his cell from his jeans.

"He did my parents landscaping," Tessa was murmuring. "I went for rides in his truck. He took all of us for rides."

Neither Tommy nor Debra heard her. Debra has collapsed into the front seat of her car and she was sobbing as she fumbled for her phone. Tommy was shouting directions into his phone. Tessa stared back at the old truck, its engine still rumbling. Gaunt had wanted to take her and her friend Ashley to the fair one fine fall day. When he pressed them to go without telling their parents, Tessa had resisted. She insisted Ashley talk to her mother also. Gaunt told them he didn't have time to wait and maybe they would go another day.

Three days later, Ashley had disappeared while riding her bike to the park. She was never seen again. Tessa had never mentioned Gaunt and his offer of a trip to the fair. It never crossed her mind that the kind old man who gave the kids rides and often brought them suckers had anything to do with the disappearance of her friend.

When she looked into what would come to be known as the "pit of horrors" she saw something that brought it all sharply to the surface. She and Ashley had matching tee shirts. The cheery yellow tee shirt with the brightly colored parrot, dulled but still visible, had enshrouded a small body in the center of the pile of cadavers. Her body lay across the partially consumed body of an older woman clothed in a tattered dress and the remains of an apron. Her legs stuck out from beneath the dress, one bare foot half devoured, the other long gone to decay and the hunger of woodland creatures.

It would take many months before the full scope of Gaunt's crimes was known. In the end no one was certain they had found all his victims.

Gaunt Thibideaux was a man of habits. With his death, they rose to the surface.

One thousand one hundred and eight miles away in the small town of Wiley, Colorado, Elvis Patrick stared at the television news report. Then his eyes drifted to the screen door and the truck that was in his backyard. The sound of children's laughter drifted into the house from the yard on the other side of his fence.

Sighing and shaking his head he picked up the newspaper. Folding it in half he studied the advertisement. The fair was coming to nearby Oakley, Kansas. He always did enjoy a trip to the fair. In fact, he made it a habit to always go at least once when it was close to home. And everyone knew, Elvis Patrick was a man of habits.

*****

ABOUT THE AUTHOR

ELIZABETH HORTON-NEWTON *loves serial killers and all things horror. She has been this way since early childhood, much to her mother's dismay. After releasing her two full length romantic thrillers to assuage her guilt about her mother, she has returned to her original love, horror. Fascinated by the inner workings of the criminal mind, an interest strongly influenced by her father, she allowed her imagination to run wild in her tale for this anthology, "Old Habits".*

INSANITARY

Robyn Cain

It was a fine morning with an Alice blue sky and a weak yellow sun. Despite the chilly air, Henrietta decided they'd be a little adventurous and take a different route to their usual. Scruffy was never a problem on walks and easily came to 'heel' when told. Out of the choice of three that she offered him, she chose the one he responded to the most keenly with energetically wagging tail. He responded to her. 'So it's the woods is it, Scruffy? You know it's the farthest away don't you?' His enthusiasm didn't abate. Given the go-ahead, they left home for the edge of their town.

Old buildings, whether in good condition or bad, never interested Henrietta. If Scruffy hadn't stopped to start snuffling around the piles of autumnal leaf-fall, she would have passed the locked metal gates without an iota of curiosity. Waiting whilst he played, she read the various faded notices that were securely attached to the bars. She smiled at one of them.

'Listen to this. It says, "*Your shit is not welcome here.*" That's quite blunt and to the point don't you think? Good for them, eh?'

He didn't even pause to answer.

Going closer, she peered through, careful not to touch the rusted bars in case she got her clothes caught and ruined. Waif-like weeds protruded from the meandering gravel drive that was practically concealed by thick-trunked trees. And they in turn were held hostage by web-covered bushes that appeared to be interwoven with matted human hair and animal fur. Hazarding that no vehicle's wheels had disturbed the area for a good few years, she murmured, 'A road very little travelled.' Then louder to Scruffy, 'Sort of quiet around these parts isn't it?'

Again he paid no heed, but this time because he was too busy scrabbling, preparing to do his daily deed. 'Not there, Scruffy. Here.' She went to the brick wall and pointed.

'Woof!' The look in his eyes told her he was going to rebel.

'Scruffy, do it here!' Her tone said it all. Refuse and his leash would be put back on.

Emitting a whining sound, ears flattened, he obeyed. Once finished he shot off, sending the leaves flying.

'Good boy.' She laughed as he put distance between them. 'Honestly, Scruffy, anyone would think your tail was on fire!'

Shoe-pushing at the multi-coloured crisping leaves, she covered his still-steaming business and hurried after him.

With the onslaught of thirst she wondered if they ought to turn around and head back. She dug into her coat pocket for her mobile to check the time. 'Damn!' For the first time in her life she'd forgotten it. 'Scruffy, let's go back. Come on my darling,' she called and then whistled.

Everything stilled. No bird song above or ruffling of feathers overhead, or scratching for food from elsewhere. She held her breath and thought she could hear the silence breathing. Finally it was broken and she filled her lungs. 'Scruffy, where are you?'

Hearing whimpering coming from behind her, she was startled. Wondering if he'd done a loop or somehow doubled back without her noticing, she retraced her footsteps. Back at the same gates she stopped. She frowned. This time there was life on the other side.

'Scruffy!' She pushed at the gates but they didn't budge. 'How did you get there, boy?' He approached her silently. Just within reach of her, he vomited. The stench was overpowering. Hunkering, she pushed a hand through the bars to comfort him. 'My poor baby you're drooling. Don't be afraid. It's all right, we'll get you out.'

His nose was hot and dry against her fingertips. She went to stroke the underside of his chin. Instead he lowered his face. His mouth opened and closed with her hand in it. She suppressed the screams for fear of frightening him and forced soothing noises from between her lips. From between the sides of his locked jaw she saw her blood drip, leaving no trace as it seeped into the ground. As the dog chomped, crunched and gnawed, he made steady progress towards her wrist.

Her faculties dulled by the pain, she didn't register the rustling of leaves at her side, nor the licks to her free hand from a familiar tongue. Only when he whimpered did Henrietta respond by looking down. 'Scruffy.' She managed a weak stretch of her lips. Scruffy's movements became frenzied. Pushing his lips back he exposed his fangs. His whine becoming a growl, he hurled himself at his opposite, but to no avail.

On the other side it was safe, unreachable and greedily still filling his stomach.

Collapsing, Henrietta saw the penalty notice come loose. It remained upright and legible as it floated towards her. She coughed and reread: *Your shit is not welcome here.*

*****

ABOUT THE AUTHOR

While in high school, ***ROBYN CAIN'S*** *writing dreams budded and waned. Those dreams were rekindled after accomplishing a first class honours degree in English/Writing, and a PGCE. Robyn went on to complete her Masters in Creative Writing and taught English and creative writing.*

Most of Robyn's books are set in Cheshire, incorporating British and Asian cultures. Each novel is in a different genre. ***Seven Stops*** *is a contemporary fiction novel;* ***Goods By Hand*** *and its sequel,* ***Footsteps of Galatea****, are supernatural novels set in modern day; and* ***A Fine Balance****, is a crime thriller novel.* ***She Dreamed of Flash Fiction*** *and* ***Manna For Heaven*** *are collections of mixed genre short stories.* ***Devil's Crochet*** *is a collection of interwoven, supernatural stories. Other short stories by Robyn have been published in India. Robyn is currently working on the sequel to Seven Stops.*

JULIAN: THE RISE OF THE PROPHECY

Lubna Sengul

"Ten years is a long time," I say as I turn to face Lilly.

I have never been able to forget Lilly; she always appears in my dreams, her turquoise eyes iridescent like jewels. They show me a vast kingdom that I will rule someday and my subjects who will bow down in adoration. The adrenaline rush that I feel when I see her visions completely consume me. She provokes a sense of power and the thirst to rule in these dreams is beyond anything that I have ever craved. I fear my own senses. I don't recognise myself around her visions, or perhaps I do but choose to oppress it when awake? The hunger that I feel is real and overpowering, to the extent it stays with me even when I am awake.

I am, however surprised, to see her here in person.

"I see your senses have become stronger," Lilly says.

"What do you want?" I ask.

"What, no polite conversation, Julian?"

I, although have been warned to stay away from Lilly, am intrigued by her. I know I should stay away, but something inside of me is getting a better grip of my senses. I do not trust her, however I would like to hear what she has to say for herself.

"Ok, what are you after? Is that polite enough for you?" I reply.

"I just came by to say to hello, and see how our King is doing now that he is a grown man," she says.

"I'm well," I reply, still unsure about her.

"Yes, I can see that. You are looking more and more like your father."

It wasn't the first time I had heard that. Mum would say it almost daily. My eyes are the same almond shape and light brown as hers; but I have my Dad's face with a strong jaw and the long brown hair to my jawbone. I am tall as him but I am stronger than him.

"It's a shame you have to hunt like this," Lilly says, walking away.

"Like what?" I ask, following behind her.

"I mean living off animal spirits. You do know that Sofayans used to feed on human spirits?" she asks.

"I had heard," I say, still walking behind her.

"Ah, but do you know why?" she asks, turning to face me now.

I shake my head.

"The sense of power a Sofayan feels, when they inhale the spirit of a human is beyond anything they have ever experienced in any other world. You see, a Sofayan spirit is strong and had not really met its match, until Sofayans came here. The human spirit is also strong. A Sofayan would feel a powerful sense of achievement in overcoming a human spirit," Lilly says. "I'm surprised the need to have that power isn't greater in you, considering you are more Sofayan than a Danfian or a human."

Lilly's comment stings my ears, as I can feel the hunger and thirst for power. It is growing silently, and the more I dream of Lilly and the vast kingdom that I will lead, the more the hunger and thirst grows. I am able to control this side when I am around Mum and Dad, for they have a beautiful energy that calms me, but the hunger and thirst only subsides, not disappear.

"We don't live like that anymore," I reply abruptly, feeling the hunger grow. I do not like the turmoil that Lilly is able create in me.

"Hmm, even so, you can't deny what you are. You should try it. Only then will you understand," she says.

"I'm not a killer," I growl, as she projects an image of me consuming a human spirit. I'm afraid of the curiosity that such an image causes.

"Not yet. Enjoy it when the time comes," Lilly says.

She then disappears.

What did she mean by that? I didn't feel the urge to take human life, but I have started to feel a strange sense of being powerful around pure human spirits. Is that what Lilly is talking about? I feel troubled by these dreams, and now I'm fearful about Lilly's last words and what the future may bring.

I will never take a human life in that manner. Mum and Dad had taught me too well for that. But the desire that Lilly has left in me could become insatiable. I have horrible feeling that I may perhaps have to face such a day and that I would enjoy the power too much. Will I have the strength to walk away?

I feel furious at Lilly, and want to confront her and demand to know what she really wants with me. But Lilly, of course, only shows up when she feels like it, although this time I know that I will see her again sooner rather than later.

I can sense Mum coming up behind me at an alarming pace.

"Lilly was here, wasn't she? I could sense her?" Mum asks.

"Yes," I reply.

"What did she want?" Mum asks.

"I'm not sure. She said something about me being a leader of a great kingdom, and then left," I say, lying. I do not want to worry her, and I also want to process the information that Lilly has left me with.

"Why didn't you inform me about Lilly the moment you saw her?" Mum asks.

"I didn't realise I had to report my every move to you," I reply.

"Hey, what's with the attitude? I'm only concerned for you."

"I don't need to be protected. Can't you see you are suffocating me?" I say. I do feel suffocated by her ever-watchful eye, but have never said anything about it before. But now I feel like my wings are being clipped and I want to break free. Perhaps Lilly is right, maybe my parents do not want me to have what I am destined for.

"I'm sorry. I didn't know you felt that way," Mum replies, looking wounded.

I feel awful for the outburst now.

"I'm just glad you are safe. I love you, and don't want any harm to come to you. I hope you understand that," she says, hugging me.

I feel guilty. I hate this turmoil that is inside of me. It is as if there are two sides to me, constantly battling with each other. The side that craves Lilly's vision seems to grow stronger as I grow older, and it overpowers the side that belongs to my parents and their world.

I know that it is only a matter of time before I will have to choose a side.

*****

ABOUT THE AUTHOR

*After graduating in law from the University of East London, **Lubna Sengul** embarked upon a very successful career within the media/advertising industry. Ten years of experience resulted in becoming an account director at Future Media Exchange Ltd. Sengul is the author of The Danfians Prophecy, a scifi/fantasy ebook, and The Chronicles of Natasha Kahn – Solidarity, a short story of heroism and vigilante action. Sengul has also had a rehearsed play reading by Kali theatre which was part of Talkback 2015. Sengul is currently working on Julian: The Rise of the Prophecy, the sequel to The Danfians Prophecy.*

KARMIC ODDS

Mark Fine

Driving makes me hungry, you see. That evening, in desperation I'd rescued a bag of mustard & honey pretzels from behind the car's passenger seat. But wish I hadn't. With one hand on the wheel I ripped open the snack bag with my teeth. Wow, the stink that assaulted my nostrils was wretched. Faced with gagging or starving, I chose the latter. But having survived a lurid workday, the relentless trek home had only aggravated my appetite, and my mood.

Snarled in slow traffic during rush hour had become numbing. Rush hour, my foot. I was wasting away in a stagnant pool of truck fumes and sweaty panic. Now, my desperation might surprise you, but my wife's a martyr when she prepares a home-cooked meal. Totally horrid if I'm late, and boy, do the accusations fly with allegations that I'm sabotaging her cooking, and that I should try being a 'latchkey bride' stuck at home all the time. These rants are often accompanied with the cold clatter of food being served with the delicacy of a panel beater at an auto body shop.

As luck would have it, that night I did arrive late. I sang my sweetest 'Honey, I'm home' greeting in the hope of neutralizing her onslaught. But nothing. No outburst whatsoever. There stood my wife, patient, demure, even inviting. She pecked me on the cheek, placed a linen napkin on my lap when I sat for dinner, and even showed some interest in my day.

To be honest I was alarmed; quite unlike her. Look, our relationship may be lusty in bed but it was turbulent elsewhere. Both of us had grown tired of the bickering and had resolved to communicate less—not what therapists would recommend, mind you, but our truce allowed a state of civilized hostility best shared in silence.

My concern subsided as Roxanne chitchatted about this and that in a surprisingly convivial manner. Actually, it was reminiscent of my dear mother's dinner conversations—just the language was different.

Finally relaxed, I turned my attention to the mouth-watering steak fajita dish before me. Famished, I began eating, when, a fist slammed hard on the table. Bang! It almost gave me a heart attack.

"Gerhard. Stop it!" she shrieked. "I've had enough already …"

Of what, I wasn't sure.

"Damnit, look at me!" Startled, I kept my eyes away from my plate, but avoided eye contact. "How long have you lived in this country, anyway?" she demanded.

Needing a reason for her outburst, I settled on a phone conversation earlier that day. We'd skirmished over the merits of refried beans. Frankly, I don't consider this mashed, reheated concoction, more the stuff and consistency of pulpy cement, fit for human consumption. Roxanne chose to disagree and inevitably I agreed to compromise; meaning I'd be served it at supper.

Now, it's fair to say I'd been fastidiously eating my way around an ugly dollop of the mush during dinner. That must be what irritated her, I thought, especially my effort to ensure no beans touched my fajita. *Agh*, I admit my utensils were at the ready to ensure the two foods, well, one a food, the other alleged, remained separated.

For the life of me I couldn't answer her question about how long I've lived in the USA, not having bothered to keep track. Sure I could work it out, I've got enough fingers to do so, but did I really want to see that smirk on her face as I tried? No way. So I stuffed my mouth with food and took refuge in silence. That silence now a wall keeping us apart, echoing the harsh division of another wall many years ago…

Our traditional Friday family dinners were usually animated affairs, with my father going on about the absurdity of a centralized economy planned by the state. He'd be beside himself at the futility of yet another unworkable Seven-Year Plan imposed by the communist government. Within the questionable safety of our dining room, (we never knew who'd be listening), he'd complain about unrealistic production quotas and the continual exodus of talented workers.

My dear mother added sustenance to these evenings with her delicious *solyanka* soup, a family recipe of pickled vegetables and meat. Only she was able to nudge father off his anti-government bully pulpit. With a merry glint in her dark eyes she'd defuse his bleak sermons with salacious gossip heard as she queued for food, always scarce, at the local *kaufhalle*.

"Henrietta told me young master Otto has run off with that Haas girl," she'd say with a dimpled grin. If her interruptions irritated father, he never showed it, guffawing affectionately with mother and me.

But one evening it was different; ominous. I was fifteen at the time. Their silent-treatment unnerved me but I was too timid to pry, being frightened of the truth. These two dear people were my foundation and my inspiration, so all I did was stare at their faces.

Father's was unusually ashen while mother's was tight around her eyes, verging on tears.

The way they shared furtive glances freaked me. "*Ach nein*," I thought. "My *mutter* and *vater* are getting divorced." My mind gathered speed like a runaway rollercoaster with crazy scenarios: Which parent would I live with? Who would make the choice? What would those bullies at school do to me knowing I'm from a broken family? Ignoring bullies, as mother always preached, was a failed strategy.

I began to weep.

Through the tears I saw two sets of worried eyes peer at me. Now, I was more convinced my folks were hiding something important. Not surprisingly, father took the lead; but he was an invalid. The tram missed his work stop one day; recklessly he jumped off and damaged his knee, permanently. With restricted mobility, and a need to survive, father honed his intellect beyond his modest station in life, devouring books and newsprint on all matters; so much so his opinions were uncannily prescient. And so I listened, intently.

"My boy, our future in the German Democratic Republic is bleak," he said. "State Council chairman Ulbricht claims there is no intention to erect a wall. Well, I don't believe him." In a moment of rueful indulgence, he paraphrased Shakespeare's

Hamlet in perfect English, "The minister doth protest too much, methinks."

The features on father's face softened momentarily, then with seven simple words he shattered my world, "Son, it is time for you leave."

Misunderstanding, I went on the attack. "What! How dare you throw me out of the house?" Then plaintively I added, "What did I do wrong…?"

In unison two heads shook left to right, then mother spoke. "Gerhard, we love you dearly and are so proud of you. Surely you know that, but for that reason we must let you go—though it breaks our hearts. The sad truth…there is no future for you in East Germany."

To this day this life-changing moment remains a blur, yet is embossed with the utmost clarity in my memory. I'll never forget the image of seeing the shoulders of my loving parents drop as they hunched in despair.

Father then brushed sentiment aside, and demanded my attention. "Listen son, you have to leave tomorrow night." My appeal for more time was brusquely rebuffed. "Gerhard, I sense an imminent change in my bones and it is going to be ugly," said father. "If not for my crippled knee we would join you, do you understand?"

Not appreciating the chance at an enriched life just granted me, I saw nothing but my future slipping into a void. Oh, woe is me tears followed in a herky-jerky parade of sobs.

Funny, now divorce seemed a delightful prospect; at least I could have remained with one parent, swapping every two weeks with the other like poor Neele from school. However, as a refugee fleeing the oppression of communism I was to become, in effect, an orphan.

The next day was August 12, the year was 1961, when I escaped East Germany. And how wise my father proved to be. I still wonder whether he had influence inside the party apparatchik, because the following night soldiers began in force building the Berlin Wall.

Nervously I waited til dusk before fleeing to the West through a rapidly closing gap as the wall went up. Later I learned 4,130 people escaped that first day, and fortunately I was one of them. Believe me, I still thank my folks every day.

All I had with me was a twine-tied suitcase, a greasy food bag and the clothes on my back. Lots of clothes. For some reason I layered them, in part to protect me from the chill of the night; having no destination I expected to sleep outdoors, in parks and doorways. But I was a scrawny kid, so the bulky garments made me look huskier, tougher, at least from a distance. Seemingly, my survival instincts had kicked in.

A weird thing, though. As I slipped across the border I heard on a wireless the song "Runaway" playing from a nearby window. As the melody faded in the distance so did my link to those I loved. But once free, it's ironic the same Del Shannon hit was a kind of siren song, drawing me to Michigan, USA—the singer's home state. There, in the city of Frankenmuth, I found a small Bavarian community steeped in Lutheran tradition, and beer.

Possibly it was an East versus West German rivalry thing—we from East Germany considered inferior—but the distant relatives I stayed with, well, they remained distant. Oh yes, there was one exception, when we all watched President Kennedy give his "Ich bin ein Berliner" speech on TV. Such a thrill it was, I'll never forget it. I even remember the date—June 26, 1963. And to think he was killed five months later, shame, what a tragedy.

+

Gerhard never saw his family again. As innocent citizens on the wrong side of an ideological divide, his parents were interred behind 43 kilometers of wall. This manmade monolith separated freedom of thought and expression from censorship and oppression. The concrete and steel monstrosity was clad in white paint and barbed wire. The whole boondoggle was guarded by a daisy-chain of 300 watchtowers reinforced with probing searchlights. It was further armed with ruthless machinegun toting guards and blood-thirsty attack dogs, ever vigilant, monitoring the kill zone between east and west.

Effective as a physical barrier, the Berlin Wall hermetically sealed off its denizens from the economic opportunities now enjoyed by their once fellow neighbors. In order to avoid discontent the ruling regime pre-empted temptation by boarding up the windows of every building, overlooking the wall, that faced west. Inevitably these two Germanys now struck out in diametrically opposite directions; one captive and one free, as one withered the other prospered. Capricious and cruel, the wall severed families and friendships with its blunt bulk. And Gerhard's family, left behind, suffered.

Any reliable communication from behind the Iron Curtain was scarce. Though Gerhard hankered for news, when it eventually reached him it was always bad. As such he learned eleven months after the sad event that his father had succumbed to pneumonia. Desperate to check on the welfare of his widowed mother, Gerhard was initially unsuccessful, but eventually he learned she'd found refuge within her tiny Heilsarmee church. Though relieved he still worried for her as having faith took courage when state-sponsored atheism was the insisted norm.

With his father gone and his mother fading, the crutch of family paled as did Gerhard's connection to his fatherland. With no need to look back, he was determined to honor his parent's sacrifice by achieving success in the New World. Again it was the West that summoned him; but this time it was the seductive sparkle of the Pacific Ocean. Drawn by the sun, and accompanied by gilded promises in the surf's up harmonies of the Beach Boys, Gerhard headed for California.

+

Frankly, I'd had it with long cold Michigan winters and disgruntled relatives. Another winter of snot freezing in my nostrils and icicles clinging to my moustache was not on—it was time for a change.

It took four days in a coach to reach Santa Monica. The moment we arrived I headed straight for the beach. Never mind a place to stay, I felt like a kid and needed to see the waves. Must have looked like an idiot, hopping barefoot in and out of the surf, trying to avoid being 'attacked' by strands of foamy wavelets; but I didn't care, no one knew me.

That quickly changed. I met Roxanne. Apparently my childish antics amused her, "Ah-ha!" she said, twirling her sunglasses. "That's quite some dance you have there...what do you call it?"

"Oh, it's called 'The Splish-Splash.'"

The dazzling creature rewarded me with a patronizing smile and a protracted pause. This distressed me as I'd clearly failed in the swift repartee department. My only wish was to be rejected with minimum humiliation. As you know, pride is important to us Germans.

The blond pretty girl stroked her golden mane behind her right ear revealing a succulent pearled earlobe. She was taunting me with her natural beauty emanating from every pore on her glorious face. With her back to the sea, I remembered the moment I first awakened to the splendor of the female form.

The immature me stoutly resisted all things cultural, so it took some arm twisting for my parents to compel me to visit the Uffizi Gallery in Florence. Any stuffy preconceptions I held were breathlessly swept away the moment my eyes met the gorgeous vision of Sandro Botticelli's *The Birth of Venus*.

Seeing Roxanne transported me back to that moment, except she wasn't emerging from a giant sea shell, she certainly wasn't naked, and angelic figures didn't surround her. Nevertheless, the fragrance of her was breathtakingly real as it drifted toward me across the ocean breeze. And so there I stood with trousers rolled-up and damp, with my nude toes clawed in the sand, awaiting swift execution.

"I just invented it," I added, playing for time.

She paused a beat more. I took the moment to lock on to her striking hazel eyes and crisply arched brows. However, I couldn't hold it, my gaze flitted down to the girl's mouth. Then I saw it, the love-charm of the philtrum—that shallow indent above her top lip—it absolutely entranced me. But it got better, I saw the wave of her lips lift in both corners to reveal an inviting smile.

"You have an accent! I love accents," she said, gushing. "Where do you come from?"

On that beach we sat, and I told her everything.

Roxanne was naïve, in the sense she wasn't worldly. But she was a quick study; her ambitions, fantasies and expectations came from the glossy pages of Cosmo magazine. It took me a while to grasp her shape-shifting ways, a real chameleon she was. "Who is your favorite actress?" she'd ask. Let's just say I mentioned Grace Kelly; before I realized it the sexy casual beach bunny had morphed into a 50s fashion icon, all immaculately groomed with poise to match.

At first it was all wonderful. After the dour gray Michigan winters, the chameleonesque antics of my beach-tinted Roxanne were a breath of fresh air. But eventually the constant personality shifts troubled me. I began to wonder 'who *is* this woman I'm sharing my life with? Who is the real Roxanne?'

Look, I realized from the get-go she was overawed by my apparent worldliness. In this silly town I had become a kind of prized trophy for her; it was strange being perceived as exotic, when I was still the same ordinary guy, and the only thing that actually changed was where I now lived. And it wasn't only Roxanne. Even my boss later admitted he hired me because I sounded sophisticated. He suggested I should be thankful that my accent 'regarded as chopped liver back in Germany was smooth as pâté here in the USA.'

And I sure took advantage of it. Since my guttural accent, old-world courtesy and quaint customs were genuinely me, I didn't see any deceit as far as my relationship with Roxanne was concerned. And to be fair we adored each other, no matter our motivations. In fact, she was attentive and I was content; and my uncomfortable feeling of being an outsider finally evaporated.

We got married with a simple ceremony on the beach. Didn't make sense to have a big affair, as my family was close to non-existent and Roxanne remained vague about hers. After five years

I applied for U.S. Citizenship—and learned about the beauty of the Constitution and Bill of Rights versus the oppressive system back in East Germany.

The day I was sworn in as a naturalized citizen I wore the navy blue suit and garish red, white and blue polka dotted tie Roxanne had bought for the occasion. Standing proudly in front of the immigration judge, for the first time in my life I was the tallest person in a room, as 83 former Vietnam refugees joined me at the swearing-in ceremony, all of us enthusiastically waving tiny 'Stars & Stripes' flags as we recited the Pledge of Allegiance. A memorable moment, more so, because my journey to find a new homeland was finally over.

However, becoming a U.S. citizen didn't mean a vacation from everyday life. Being a husband I was determined to do well by my wife, so I got myself a job in automation technologies.

"Damnit, Gerhard!" she yelled, frustration growing. "Stop doing that…"

Still confused by the reason for Roxane's outburst, I raised my eyebrow quizzically. It only inflamed the situation further.

Both her hands began flapping about like the wings of an albatross struggling to take flight. *Oh, we are going to mime, are we? Well, at least that's better than shrieking at one another.*

Then the cross-hatched sawing motion of her hands came clear to me. I understood. Chastened, like a kid, I carefully placed my eating utensils down, either side of my plate.

Too be clear, I may now be an American but the traditions of my youth remain with me. In European style I hold the cutlery, or flatware as it's called here, in both hands as I eat. None of that up-tools, down-tools stuff, swapping hands when eating.

Confession time: it amused me no end watching Roxanne chase food—let's say green peas, around her plate, jabbing at them with her fork. Or how she'd pre-cut food into bite sized chunks, as a parent would for child, before swapping the fork to her right hand for the big scoop. Or the way she violently mashed food with the side of a fork in an effort to cut it, when a perfectly sharp knife sat right beside her plate.

"I've had it up to here with your tiresome habits," Roxanne said, giving a harsh salute to her throat. "It's so pretentious." Now I admit the slight hurt, but damn, I had no idea a word like 'pretentious' was in her lexicon.

"But it's correct," I pleaded. "It's not some mindless affectation." Speaking of affectation, it struck me that I missed my favorite affectation of hers, the way she swept her hair behind her ear.

"Why after all these years do you insist being so odd?" she asked, "It's bloody annoying."

That was the moment I should have realized I'd overstayed my welcome. My international ways, until now a virtue, were inexplicably the source of Roxanne's frustration. With nothing more to say I picked up my knife and fork and continued with the meal. Though raw onions offend and bell peppers uncooked are so-so, when both are seared with meat the caramelized aromas do delight my palate, and thus I savored the moment despite the raging storm overhead.

As the debris of supper was scraped into the trash, hostilities faded. In a sweet please-do-me-a-favor voice, Roxanne asked, "Honey, would you run over to 7/11 and buy *us* a Lotto ticket? Can you believe the pool's reached fifty-seven million dollars?"

"*Häh*," I said, surprised by both the request and the size of the pot.

Roxanne scrawled six numbers on a pink pad next to the phone. She ripped off the top sheet, protectively folded it, and pushed it into my palm—almost conspiratorially. "Quick, before the deadline closes," were the last words I heard as the door shut behind me.

I remember wondering what witchcraft my wife used to conjure up these specific numbers. Throughout our relationship she'd bemuse me with her psychic dabbling; first it was our daily horoscope—she Sagittarius and me Cancer—and all went swimmingly until she discovered our signs were, well, not compatible. Apparently the great oracle in the sky foretold our relationship was 'troublesome.' Then came *I Ching*. This irritated me because every important family decision was then made based on the toss of three coins.

Eventually, Roxanne graduated to a fortune teller located next to a bikini boutique. Even with the 'Always Open' neon sign lit in the window I was never open to visiting the soothsayer despite Roxanne's incessant nagging. I took it all with a pinch of salt.

Thinking back I should have made the effort—not because I was into that gobbledygook, but it would've been wise to know more about this stranger that had such influence over the decisions our family made; more influence than even me. However, I let things be, after coming from a restrictive society who was I to interfere in someone else's kooky beliefs?

Agh, I've digressed. Where were we again? Oh yes, wondering what six numbers Roxanne had chosen. One thing: they'd be odd numbers because Roxanne was superstitious that way; she's totally convinced odd numbers are luckier than even.

Hmm, it just occurred to me she chose an even year for us to get married.

Look, I'm no gambler—too pragmatic for that—so I avoid routinely playing Lotto. But, if buying coffee and I have a spare dollar handy, I'd put it on a random Quick Pick. Never won anything, though. However, that evening I entered Roxanne's six numbers on the ticket and paid the one dollar. Then I did something quite unusual for me. I prayed. Not sure why, maybe due to the wicked odds of this so-called game of chance; 1 in 13,983,817 *against* even getting back a wooden nickel.

I rushed home to find Roxanne seated with the TV remote gripped in her hand. There was a knowing gleam in her eyes. After a quick cross-examination confirming I'd indeed purchased the ticket, Roxanne patted the cushion beside her and I joined my wife on the settee.

A glib television announcer, dressed in a too-tight tuxedo, was accompanied on the flickering screen by his lovely, ever smiling cohost. But my focus was on the Rube-Goldberg contraption placed on an altar at center stage. To me the gadget looked like the progeny of an otherworldly romantic liaison between a vacuum cleaner and a gumball machine. However, the hosts fawned over it as if it was some mystical totem from the New Church of Random Providence. And so with great reverence the talisman sucked up several numbered ping pong balls in a sonic chorus of *whooooschts… whooooschts.* Then, as though a charismatic call to the faithful, the TV host recited the final selections, "7…9…27…29…33…and…47!"

"ALLRIGHT!" she shrieked. "I totally knew it!" Roxanne was ecstatic. Grinning, she swept strands of golden hair behind both ears and turned toward me.

"Why, that's unbelievably wonderful," I said, the grin on my face striving to match hers. Difficult to do considering her luscious mouth is as generous as mine is sparse. (Dentists detest laboring in the confined space despite the healthy reward they've gotten for replacing all my primitive East German fillings.)

Heck, my mind was reeling in an effort to absorb what just happened. It was so improbable. But there was Roxanne twirling about our twill carpet, full of the joy of winning.

I admit I was swept up in the moment. "Come darling," I said, "let us celebrate."

"What do you mean *us*?" hissed Roxanne. "From now on it's all about *me*."

"But Roxanne…" I got no further.

She went on about how dull I was, what a disappointment I'd been, how I'd never ever taken her overseas, and didn't I realize she'd never even been out of California.

Devastated, I reached out in an effort to still the bile, and to reassure her. "Surely you don't mean it?" I pleaded. "I adore you."

"That's not half of it, buster! Your weirdo habits drive me nuts. And shut up, it's irritating." Roxanne's hand snaked out, "Now give me that ticket," she demanded.

Without protest I gave it over.

"Hang on. I'll be right back," she said, then disappeared into our bedroom. Roxanne returned with a large manila envelope. I was instructed to read it, immediately, in front of her. I ripped it open. To say I was stunned is an understatement; I'd just been served divorce papers.

"Now that's dealt with, the Lottery winnings are all mine," said Roxanne, with a smirk.

She turned her attention to the lottery ticket. As Roxanne read out the numbers her voice cracked with dismay, "**1**…9…**21**…29…33…4**1**!"

Manically she repeated the process, again and again—punching at the card as she read, as if doing so would alter the outcome. With sobering realization, tears began sluicing down her cheeks in oily streaks of blackened mascara.

"Three of them are all wrong!" cried Roxanne. "Where have all the 'sevens' gone?"

"That's odd?" I said. "I know I filled in the exact numbers you gave me. I even checked it twice."

"How dare you do this to me, you moron," she responded. I was about to take issue with this but the next thing out of Roxanne's mouth was a revelation, "This can't be happening…? My fortune teller gave me those numbers. She swore they were right."

I was stunned. That fortune teller was no charlatan. She'd actually summoned up the correct six numbers; quite extraordinary, really. But the fact Roxanne was the architect of her own destruction appeared mightier to me, as though some other force was balancing the odds. And so I began to explain it all to my soon-to-be ex-wife.

"Hmmm, pity you never bothered to appreciate my way of doing things." Seeing the confusion on her face, I added, "You see in Germany, when we write, we cross the number 'seven' in the middle." As there was little comprehension in those caked mascara eyes, it was necessary to continue. "The reason we do this is to avoid confusing 'seven' with the number 'one'. After all, we don't want to make any silly mistakes, now do we?"

I know this seems patronizing, but she'd hurt me, and I needed some measure of vindication.

With a black pen I carefully wrote on the reverse side of the now useless lottery ticket two numbers in the accepted German and European style: **17–**

"So you see Roxanne, if you'd simply crossed your sevens like I do—and you've seen me do this a million times over the years—it would've been impossible for this mix up to happen."

"But, we live here in America, it's not my fault," she said, petulant. Roxanne tilted her head as if attempting to clear cobwebs; a few strands of hair fell away from behind her right ear.

"No Roxanne, your mistake is double-times worse." I then laid it on thick. "You see that small tail at the top of the German 'one', well that was your second clue? Don't you agree it resembles the 'seven' you scribbled on the note you gave me?"

"But…," bleated Roxanne.

"No *buts* about it, Roxanne. Clearly, anyone can see this was entirely your mistake."

I stood there quietly and watched that beautiful face dissolve into a shadowed caricature. The metamorphosis was a dark echo of all those fake personalities she'd adopted during our time together. The collapse of her vanity must have pained her first; then it must have been the realization that she'd been outplayed, not only by my dull, methodical habits, but by ignoring her latest mystical pursuit—a trendy Californication of the revered doctrine, Buddhism.

Apparently Roxanne had missed the memo about moral causation, and that for past actions an individual will in time receive what they deserve. Or, more likely Roxanne felt exempt from any form of self-reflection; and why should she, she had a fortune teller in her corner.

But for me it was a moment of pure wonderment, especially the irony of it all. How could someone so shallow receive such tangible manifestations of her ersatz beliefs; having both the winning Lotto numbers predicted and getting served immediate retribution for her unkind actions, yet somehow bungled it all so badly?

It was very odd, it could only be explained by her karma.

+

Okay, I've come to accept that karma had something to do with it. However, that evening as I entered that 7/11 market next to the laundromat I admit to being irritated by Roxanne's insults at dinner, but revenge was the furthest thing from my mind as I had no knowledge of her deceitful divorce plans. As for the winning lottery numbers, it was so wildly improbable I couldn't possibly have anticipated it, or planned for it.

As if it was yesterday I remember the glass doors swing shut behind me, and the toxic fumes of dry cleaning solvents and pungent ammonia being replaced with the all-American smell of hotdogs sweating on the grill. Heaven! We Germans are into our sausages. Having had dinner I wasn't hungry, but indulging in a Slurpee was another matter. Guzzling this crushed-ice and syrup concoction had become for me an act of subversion. Not that Roxanne ever knew of my rebellion despite mocking me for my beer belly, not realizing my sweet tooth was the culprit. *He-he*, the skinny kid that crawled through a gap in the Berlin Wall would've gotten stuck today.

Sucking the thick red straw carefully, to avoid the dreaded brain freeze, I unfolded Roxanne's pink note and noticed three numbers shared a common characteristic. That's when I changed them; it was a spur of the moment thing—just to annoy her, just to teach her a lesson for mocking me.

Can you imagine my shock when her actual numbers won? I felt so guilty. But that vanished when she blindsided me with that greedy divorce stuff. Also, I paid for that lottery ticket, not

Roxanne. Thank goodness. If it was her dollar, I'd be the one saddled with the karmic conscience.

+

My last memory of Roxanne was the crushed lottery ticket held in a fist against her chest—now completely useless due to the cultural myopia and meanness-of-spirit of her own making. Sometimes I wonder if she still thinks I fooled her, or that it was nothing more than a genuine mistake by a stranger from a strange land.

I guess she will never know.

*****

ABOUT THE AUTHOR

Author ***MARK FINE*** *was a label chief for PolyGram records. Variety magazine named him "Music Executive with 20/20 Vision"—good thing too as Fine is chronically tone-deaf. In an effort to beat his affliction Fine has tried to compose his first song. Met with failure he wrote, instead, the critically acclaimed novel,* The Zebra Affaire*. As research for his 'Karmic Odds' story Fine immigrated to America from South Africa, in an effort to better appreciate being a stranger in a strange land. Readers may follow his efforts to finally write a song, or his next book with the working title,* ***The Hyena Axis****, via his websites listed below or Twitter:* @MarkFine_author.

www.TheFineMaxim.com

www.MarkFinebooks.com

LETTING GO

Michelle Medhat

He scrunched it up. Every element of energy absorbed into the pulp profiling a pathetic perfunctory past. It made a little sound. A light call of recognition, but Simon refused acknowledgement. He pressed tight, embedding it into his palm; the folds overlapping erratically, without logic. Origami practiced by a drunk. He stared, drawn hypnotically to its form, as if a latent power exuded. Maybe once.

So tiny; a white rose head in his hand. A stationery beauty. His fingers closed over it and it vanished. Contents extinguished; its life no more. A simple trick by sleight of hand. His mouth sloped into a sneer. A hand that'd been capable of much more…

When she requested a private meeting, he thought she suspected. Something in her voice. A gentleness, he'd not heard before. With a touch of regret. Just a whisper, but sufficient to indicate her fluency in the facts he knew.

Lunchtime. The restaurant had been packed. Simon wanted seclusion, away from interrogative eyes, but the meeting's timing had prevented such privacy. Waiting, he watched others, slipping surreptitious sideways glances from behind the menu. Couples touching with tentative affections; prickly pin-stripes doing deals, ladies who lunch scanning the room voraciously for their next meal ticket. All peacocks preening and posturing with pompous delight.

"Hello, thanks for coming."

Wrapped up in his supercilious surveillance, Simon failed to notice her approach. As usual, she leapt into her overpowering tone of effusive excitement.

"Sorry I was late, just had a couple of things to sort out."

"No problem," muttered Simon, masking signs of his anxiety.

"I thought I'd see you here instead of the office. Somehow, it didn't feel right to do it there."

"Do what there?" questioned Simon, although now he was surer than ever of the answer.

She looked down. Her eyes avoided his. She glanced to the left of him. Her breath came out heavier. Simon recognised her unease. He hoped release would unburden her.

She took a deep breath. Appeared to retreat inside herself for a moment. Simon watched. She breathed out. Her emotions centred, she was ready.

She turned her beautiful eyes direct on Simon.

"Look, you're a great sales executive. You really came in on target, but things are changing. Market consolidation means there's less players, but also opportunities are shrinking. Times are getting tougher. We've got to streamline to stay ahead, you know what I'm saying."

Mary smiled. The mouth that once appeared warming now waned its inner glow. A red rip on a fraudulent face.

"I…I…don't understand?" stuttered Simon.

"Oh come on, you know how it is in this business, last one in, first one out. I feel bad about this, as I took you under my wing, saw your potential. But business is business. Anyway, you're what, twenty four, twenty five? Good track record, decent degree, know the tricks, you won't have to wait long. That phone will soon be ringing. So, what are you having? They do a great seared scallops…"

Simon was caught; transfixed by her nonchalance. Her dismissive demeanour expressing her denouncement: that he was nothing more than work fodder, and that scallops were more worthy of her attention. He wanted to speak, to say the words that spiked cruelly like cactus needles on his tongue. But a mute state gripped him. The waiter glared expectantly, his pen poised to pad.

"Simon, you gonna order. You know I can't be late, got the Board meeting this afternoon. I'll order for you. He'll have the…"

"Wait!"

Simon heard a man's voice, loud, powerful and defiant. The man was shouting. Mary stopped ordering and stared embarrassed by Simon's interjection.

"You're letting me go!"

"Of course…I thought you…"

"You're really letting me *fucking* go!"

"Simon, I thought what I said was obvious, now order and don't make a scene."

"You don't even know who I am, do you? After all this time. And you still don't have a clue."

Mary looked confused. Simon could see he'd disrupted her plans. A nice little get together, and then get lost, as per Mary's usual modus operandi with those past their sell-by date.

"I'm sorry…?"

"No, I'm sorry…for spending three years of my life with a heartless bitch like you."

Simon grabbed his coat, his actions uncoordinated, and he collided with another diner as he left at speed. The restaurant's ambience had become oppressive, claustrophobic. On departure, all eyes were upon him.

"Don't be like this, you're not a child!"

Simon span round, confronting Mary, who had followed him out. With eyes streaming salty hot tears, he shouted: "No, but I was once!"

His voice trembled, on every syllable his hopes broke apart. He watched Mary regard him. Cold eyes made for business. The 'shaft you as soon as look at you' stare that had delivered the edge to her in the dog-devour-dog world of high pressure media sales.

"We were all children once, Simon. You're not making any sense."

"Life doesn't make any sense," replied Simon, now calmer. Realisation had set in. A finality he dared not let enter his mind had somehow inveigled in by stealth; a cheap crook looking to destroy his possessions.

"I'm only letting you go," said Mary, exasperated. Her discomfort at being unable to read Simon concealed with professional swiftness. "You behaving like this. Well, is it about something else? I am *only* letting you go."

He listened, the brusqueness, the icy disdain that crept into her clipped voice. She had no idea at all. Probably, never even thought about it. Just another process; a quick off-loading and on to other things. More *important* things.

"You're letting me go AGAIN!"

He said it, and stared at her, praying for some reaction. A flash of recognition. Anything that could define a semblance of humanity in her selfish soul. But her cold eyes narrowed, a mean smirk defaced her chiselled features.

"What the hell are you talking about? Have you gone mad?"

Words of closure. He knew then it was over. All the fantasies he'd had. All the moments he'd imagined of a sweet, gentle reunion. Now, but fragments, shattered; mirror pieces each reflecting a reality not quite whole.

"You don't really know."

His eyes darkened, as he recited the contents he'd lived with for 5 years: "St Thomas' Hospital, London, 17 July 1990."

It all came back, thrusting forward through the murky depths of her mind. Through the godless grime that made up her life after it happened. A date and place eradicated from existence reincarnated on Simon's spoken word.

Mary shivered. Cold slithered through her, as memories stormed the outpost on the far reaches of her consciousness.

It had started a really cool party. Her best friend Kirsty had arranged everything. She wanted it to be an 'unforgettable 16th'. Ambition accomplished.

"Hey Mary, try this one."

She'd persisted a lifetime in rendering that invitation to silence, but still his call echoed on relentless. Laughing, she knocked back the drink, to the familiar cheers of "Go for it!" She woke, groggily to the same sounds, same cheering; different room. Faces lurched, elongated and surreal around her. She sensed movement. Her body was undulating, but she was paralyzed. Gradually, her vision focused. She saw him. And felt him. Deep inner pain. His face elated as he thrust with savage ferocity into her. She opened her mouth and screamed. His tight balled fist came toward her and darkness was her sanctuary.

She had the child. Her strict Catholic parents, who never discovered the truth behind her pregnancy, would not have accepted abortion. They were distraught enough by her loaded revelation of pregnancy. Mary didn't want to make them suffer further.

Mary looked at him with utter contempt and hate. She couldn't bear to share the same air with him. He moved forward, and she recoiled.

"You despise me, don't you?"

Mary was numb. Unable to believe that Simon was the product of that night. Terrified to confront the past, she backed away, edging down the narrow alley.

"Am I so terrible?" called Simon, watching her retreat.

His voice, she'd never realised. The monster's voice. His eyes, the same sinister eyes that had enjoyed those stolen views. The same hands that had delivered her ignominy; her shame.

She'd never noticed the similarities. Until now.

"You let me go once, there won't be a second time," Simon screamed, insane with hurt, and charged at Mary, pushing her against the wall. Terror reflected in her eyes. He enjoyed the moment. He revelled in the uncustomary vulnerability sudden shock had brought upon her. His hand forced her head back, slamming it hard on the brick. For a second, her eyes flickered, and then her body thudded to the floor. Crimson twisted through her blond hair.

Mary struggled to speak. She whispered: "Simon, you don't understand. I had no choice…"

Simon glared, droplets of pure hatred glistened in his dark eyes.

"I understand, Mother. You had a choice, but you just wanted to throw me away."

"No it wasn't…" But Mary's energy dissipated before she could finish. Without remorse, Simon turned away from the lifeless lump that graced the ground.

He opened his hand. It was still there. The birth certificate hadn't vanished as he'd thought. Simon threw it with precision towards a destination designed to receive it. The bin welcomed the deposit.

After all, it was only another piece of rubbish.

*****

ABOUT THE AUTHOR

MICHELLE MEDHAT *has had an exciting career that spans over 27 years in technology, science, education and marketing. Currently, Michelle is Director of Operations and Strategic Development at NEF: The Innovation Institute, an educational charity and professional institute that she co-founded with her husband Professor S Sam Medhat in 2004. The Institute has donated millions of pounds to the science, engineering and technology education sector, and has helped to improve the lives of over 600,000 people.*

*In her spare time, Michelle enjoys writing, reading, painting and singing. During her career, she has written extensively for publications, journals and newspapers, and has numerous short stories published in various anthologies. Michelle has two published books—**Connected: The Call** and **Connected: The Shift**.*

PRIME MERIDIAN

Geoff Nelder

Tuesday

He was looking at the sky watching the contrails of Malaga bound 747s. Brave single-engine planes zigzagged beneath, keeping to lower horizontal layers like sparrows wary of higher eagles. He should've been urging on pupils from his year ten form and if he had, they might have absorbed some inspiration and turned their near miss into victory. He shivered his perfunctory support, looking forward more to the tea and biscuits only a short walk away at his home.

He looked at his pupils gathering their remaining energies for the final surge against a superior side.

"Are you glad you came, sir?"

"What? Oh yes, Charlene, of course," he lied as he pulled his John Barry coat tighter against the November chill. His mother told him he was too thin to withstand proper winters.

"Come on Brad, put your effing boot in!"

"Hey, watch your language," he said, demonstrating adult shock.

"Oh, it's expected, sir, let it all out." She leapt up and down, demonstrating in her turn, teenage female energy making him feel tired. He was glad to hear the final whistle.

He had to brew his own tea, being both single and new to the area. He'd recently inherited the Victorian end of terrace in Cavendish Road, Chingford from his grandfather. Then he'd discovered that Chingford Borough High School needed maths teachers. They were so desperate they employed him, John Forrister, who used his six-feet-eight height as a discipline aid.

He put the kettle on. The bottle of Grants pulled at him but he resisted for another hour, in order to get the ticks and crosses in more or less the right places. There was an in-pile of lesson books at his feet plus the one on his lap. Throwing the latest marked effort at the out-pile and sending it spilling on the old Axminster carpet revealed something he'd not noticed. A cigarette burn mark stared defiantly at him. He thought he'd covered all his granddad's carpet-despoiling indiscretions. He didn't really like the house, whose features included being musty, draughty, creaked when he tried to sleep, but his income wouldn't let him change much for a while. The only uplifting experience was the evening view from his bedroom when he could, habitually, see the neighbour in her penthouse bedsit washing her hair, apparently not wanting to get any of her clothes wet.

He toppled books as he knelt on the carpet to examine the mark. Maroon tufts were singed in a thumbnail-sized disfigurement. Mild puzzlement turned to surprise when his finger found itself worming through a hole in the floorboard beneath. He sat on the floor, his legs either side of the hole, and tried to think how he missed the hole before but his head hurt from the effort.

He was hungry so he rang for a take-away pizza instead.

Wednesday

He couldn't leave school when the beasts fled the building, on account of departmental meetings—inspections next term. He managed to keep his eyes open until hitting the pavement home at five.

This time the bottle of Grants whisky lost mass as it went towards nerve steadying. He sat heavily at the pre-war wooden kitchen table. It wasn't fair that he was expected to rewrite schemes of work, syllabuses, remark books properly, replace the curled up wall-displays and cultivate some boot licking skills as backup.

He was drumming his fingers on the table, trying not to think how to prioritise his tasks, when his right index finger became stuck in a hole. Not properly stuck, just enough to be pulled out easily and to make him quiz his finger. He'd not come across any knotholes in the table when he spray-polished it on Sunday. Maybe he was drumming too hard and the knot fell through. Knocking through a knot with his finger was unlikely, giving it sufficient force to go through the floorboards as well was just ridiculous, even in his foul mood. But there it was. He lay on his stomach under the table fingering the newly discovered hole in the linoleum. It travelled through the floorboard like the carpet hole. Had he inherited a house with the largest woodworm in Britain? He rolled over onto his back to get a different viewpoint of the hole in the table. He could see a clean hole in the table as a white disc of light. With a little squinting, he could peer through it to the tall white ceiling. It had its own hole.

Breathlessly charging up the stairs, he found a hole in the boxroom's yucky-green lino. It drew his eyes upwards. There it was: another hole. It went on. He'd not been up in the attic; didn't know how. A much-painted-over trapdoor tried to hide in the corridor ceiling but no ladder; and he'd enjoyed too much whisky to consider rearranging his furniture into a pyramid.

He was sufficiently compos mentis to lie on the boxroom lino and, while coating his sweatshirt with floor fluff, peeped down the hole to the rest of his house. The holes didn't line up vertically. His finger told him and his eye confirmed the slight angle. He had to rule out oversized woodworm unless it had a laser guidance system. His whisky-fuddled synapses gave up for the night.

Thursday

He was obliged to look up at the sky at the end of the school day. Unnaturally ear-splitting explosions and a riot of ever expanding umbrellas of lights filled the sky in overlapping waves. It was November 5th, Guy Fawkes Day, when Britons celebrate either the attempt to blow up parliament or the success of thwarting the conspiracy. Maybe his holes were made with pre-emptive firework rehearsals. In which case they might've stopped turning his house into a colander by now. It was late when he reached his doorstep. He didn't relish finding more holes, and other staff from the school-supervised firework display helped him spend a good portion of his salary at the Fox & Hounds. He was aiming his front door key when a young lady's voice cut the air behind him.

"Mr Forrister?"

"It might be," he said, trying to stop the alcohol in his breath escaping. "Who wants to know?"

"I'm Teresa Czeremchka." She spoke with a Polish accent. "I live in the top flat next to your house."

He thought he'd recognised her face as that at the penthouse window, and if she'd seen him through wet hair on those occasions it could explain why she wasn't smiling.

"John. I'm John. Would you like to come in for a drink?"

"No. I have to tell you about your roof."

"My roof? Oh I suppose you can see it from your window. Interesting view is it?"

"Not as interesting as yours, I think," she replied with a straight face. "I saw damage to your roof the other afternoon."

He sobered immediately. "Was it Tuesday by any chance?"

"Yes. A quarter past three."

"What can you see up there?"

"Broken tiles."

"I don't suppose you saw it happen?"

"I think it was what you call a shooting star? It glowed."

"My God, I'm under attack from outer space! Have you seen more of them?"

"I don't spend all my time watching your house."

"I didn't mean to …' he blurted, "but I'd be grateful if you'd tell me –"

"I intend to buy curtains, Mr Forrister."

He heated with embarrassment about his incidental peeping but his thoughts were more on the shooting star and any more holes he might find inside. He'd heard of extinction size asteroids landing but thought shooting stars burnt up in the atmosphere. He couldn't find a fresh hole so went to make a coffee. Damn, his sink overflowed of today's breakfast crockery and yesterday's curry supper. Cursing his sloppiness he lifted the saucepan and dropped it when a jagged hole told him he didn't need to clean it anymore.

Lifting the pan again revealed the hole's continuation into the stainless steel, making it the only sink in Chingford with two plugholes. Upstairs he found it had also whizzed through his grandfather's grandfather clock. It had stopped at three fourteen.

Lying in bed he wondered how safe it was to stay. The one consolation was that whatever made the hole, shooting stars or wayward fireworks—unlikely—it only happened once a day. He should've worried himself awake longer but the alcohol took over.

Friday

Suppose it was rock fragments hurtling into his house: which organisation do you report it to? The police, his insurance company, the Royal Astronomical Society? Alan Cooper. As head of physics at Chingford Borough High, he was the ideal man to investigate his house: right up his street.

"No, man, not shooting stars, they're meteors and don't land. Meteorites are the ones; they're brilliant, John. It'll be meteorites landing on your house. That's fantastic!"

"Glad you're so pleased. But I thought meteorites landed about once every century or so."

"A meteorite the right size to make a hole to fit your finger lands every twenty minutes," said Cooper.

"My God," Forrister said, looking up at the sky as they walked to his house.

"That's for the whole planet of course. An area the size of London gets a hit of a pea to a grape-size meteorite every three years."

"You'll have to readjust your figures 'cos my house gets one every day."

"Ah."

"Ah?"

"Well, it could happen, you know, swarms; but they're usually seen as meteors like the Leonids, which are fragments of comets. They're over within twenty-four hours."

"If it's not meteorites, maybe it's one of them?" Forrister said, pointing at the lights of an aircraft heading towards Luton.

"Could be; but I wouldn't rule out meteorites until I get one in my hands. What do they look like?"

"Haven't a clue, that's why you're coming down into my basement with me to sort out the meteorites from the meteorwrongs."

"Haha, your basement so unruly you can't see recent additions?"

"Only been down once to see where I could put a wine rack but there's too much junk. I've only been there two months."

"Been in mine twenty years and still haven't sorted the cellar, assuming I have one," Cooper said.

They searched but couldn't find any new holes. They shouldered the stiff door to the cellar but it was a near-hopeless task, finding the culprits in the assorted boxes and piles of mostly metal junk.

"Your granddad an engineer?"

"Yeah, he had a workshop down here making one-twentieth scale steam engines. Hence all the swarf and black metallic lumps. If they were meteorites what are we looking for?"

"Pieces of black metallic lumps," Cooper said, glumly.

Giving up, they sat in the lounge, each with a Fosters.

"So today's hasn't happened. Yet you think they all happen around three fifteen. Today's could be late so I'll stop a while."

"Should we be wearing tin hats?"

"They'd hit the roof at around four hundred miles an hour and after going through the attic would slow considerably, with each floor, taking a fraction of a second to get to the basement. If your floors weren't Victorian cheapo wood they would get lodged en route."

"Hope it stops soon, my insurance won't pay for meteorite hits."

"That's right; but they would if they came from satellites or aircraft, and I've been coming round to thinking there must be a Wright Brothers seven-four-seven up there popping rivets on a regular basis," Cooper said.

Forrister shook his head. "I can't find a flight that takes off or lands on time every day that might account for the holes."

"Assuming your neighbour and the clock time wasn't coincidental, it seems unlikely that human timetabled events were responsible for such accuracy. On the other hand some artefacts have to be very accurate."

"Such as satellites?"

"Exactly, although there's hundreds of them up there and at least four hundred defunct ones; but, apart from the minibus-sized ones, which are well plotted, whole ones completely burn up. Something else relating to satellites might be happening though," he said, drifting off into deep thought.

"Another can?"

"Thanks. You live in an interesting scientific location you know."

"No I don't. It's Chingford."

"It's also on the Greenwich Meridian, you know, zero degrees longitude."

"Yeah, but so are lots of places," Forrister said.

"Apart from Greenwich and a few other London streets, there is no other city in England or anywhere else in the world precisely on the Prime Meridian. Look at an atlas, John."

"Don't need to with you around."

"Well I did some post-grad research on Meteosat and guess which line of longitude it's on?"

"Mine, I presume."

"Yes, zero; but also dead over the equator, whereas we are considerably farther north."

"But if something was being ejected or knocked off Meteosat it doesn't mean the bits would land on the same latitude, surely?"

"You're right: it must just be an amazing coincidence but," Cooper drifted off again, "on the other hand…"

"Maybe there's something mystic about the Prime Meridian– like ley lines. Anyway, it's two a.m. and no space debris callers. I've got to find a roof repairer tomorrow."

"Yeah, I'll give you a ring over the weekend if I think of anything. Hey, maybe you should stay at my place until it stops."

"It might've stopped already."

"Or it might've called and got lodged in a deep joist."

"I'll take my chances since they only come in the afternoons."

"I'll be off," goodbyed Cooper. He stood and turning to collect his coat, noticed the cushion he'd been squashing all evening.

"Er, John, do you usually keep your cushions in this state?" He raised a green braided lump becoming inside out via two holes. They looked up at the second hole in the lounge ceiling, wondered what it had drilled upstairs, and then examined the chair.

"At least it must've happened before you sat down," Forrister said.

"That's what you think," joked Cooper, feeling for holes over his body.

Saturday

He blinked at the late morning sun as he creaked open his half-glazed front door.

"You need to repair your roof, Mr Forrister."

"Oh hello, Miss Creze, Crzenchk–"

"Miss Czeremchka. Did your beer-soaked brain take in what I said?"

"Sorry? I'm not drunk—that was last night. No, I don't do drunk anymore, Miss Cz…it's Teresa isn't it?"

"Miss Czeremchka to you. I know a builder who do a temporary roof repair for you."

"Really, that's brilliant. I visit my mother on Sundays…"

"Orpington?"

"Yes, but how do you know?"

"I … I knew your grandfather. He needed someone to get his shopping and the odd job in-between your rare visits."

"I had no idea. He was so stubborn, insisting on living alone until the end and I lived up north. I should be thanking you."

"I liked him, he was more polite. I could let the builder in for you if it has to be Sunday."

"That's brilliant, let me give you a spare key."

"I have one. Your grandfather gave it me."

Curiosity overcame his fear when he returned from Savaspend with plastic bag handles cutting into both hands. Dumping them in the corridor he ran down into the basement. He knew it was the safest place; and he saw a Second World War air-raid warden helmet he was going to wear.

He sat down on an old swivel chair and looked at his watch: 3:11. Just in time to hear a low frequency crump noise upstairs, followed by more sounds, including one sounding like his front door banging. Fearful, he looked up at the wooden cellar ceiling, waiting for a meteorite to come through. Nothing. Puzzled, he went up the cellar steps, seeing snowflakes of plaster flutter down from a hole in the ceiling. He cursed when he saw baked beans splattered over the corridor wall and floor. The meteorite must be buried in the foundations next to the cellar after neatly puncturing the Savaspend carrier and baked beans as if it knew just where to maximise clearing up time.

Sunday

It was a difficult visit for John Forrister. Clockwise congestion on the M25 didn't help. His comatose aged mother, however, allowed his mind to go into orbit, where it worried about waking up one morning with a hole in one of his vital bits.

It was three-twenty so he'd survived another day.

His mobile phone nearly jumped out of his pocket. Alan Cooper.

"Any more incoming?"

"Yesterday not back in today."

"I've had an email reply from a Canadian geophysicist who's interested in your house."

"It's his for two hundred grand."

"I didn't mean…hey that's a bit cheap, John."

"Not for a Swiss cheese you have to keep out of at quarter past three every day."

"Anyway my friend reckons they could be tektites."

"What tights? Sounds like hosiery."

"They're ejecta from volcanoes. They can travel far from eruptions like from Etna for instance."

"Size and colour? Time of impact?"

"Often look like shiny black buttons or beans. Usually land within a day of eruptions and of course Etna's been throwing up regularly for a while. On the other hand it's not likely for tektites to whiz over one at a time although bursts of activity can happen at precise intervals. There's likely to be a swarm of them. Have you heard of any others in your area?"

"I haven't got to know many neighbours yet, apart from one."

"Have a look around then, there should be what they call a strewn field. See you at the zoo tomorrow, yeah?"

"Where? Oh yeah right, bye," Forrister said, reaching his house.

Two men were collapsing a ladder, the top part scratching its way down the gable end of his house. The larger of the two men looked at Forrister, hitched up his forty-two inch trousers, wiped a hand across his lived-in moustache, and holding out the same hand, stepped forward.

"Mr Forrister?"

"Yes. Much damage up there?" he said, now wiping his own hand on his trousers.

"Seen worse."

"Oh? Not lots of broken tiles then?"

"Looks like your roof's never been maintained, one biggish hole where rain would've wet your attic, and it looked as if whoever put your TV aerial up had studs on his boots."

"That'd be tektite damage," Forrister said, instantly regretting it.

"You what?"

"I mean meteorites," he explained, making matters worse.

"You what?"

"Is it all right now then?"

"Oh no, they don't make those tiles any more; and it'd take a while to order re-cycled ones, then a couple of days work to fix it proper. I've tarpaulined the one biggish hole and fiddled the others so you won't get wet."

"Thanks," Forrister said, worried about escalating costs if he had to reroof every other Sunday for ever. "By the way Mister er…"

"Cadogan, Grant Cadogan, here's me card—the phone number's wrong."

"Thanks, Mr Cardigan, but let me know before you shin up your ladder again won't you? Oh, and just out of interest, have other roofs had any damage around here recently?"

"Funny you should ask that," Cadogan said.

"There have been other roofs?"

"There's always a few each year near the railway and the school, both caused by kids: they put scrap on the tracks. The bits sometimes get flicked up in the air—quite spectacular. Varmints. Used to do it meself. Be seeing you, Mr Forrister."

It hadn't occurred to him about kids. The railway and the school: his house was close to both. So: railway, school, flight paths of two major airports and a couple of local ones, not to mention the Greenwich or Prime Meridian. A snag was the timing. He could easily check on the railways, but it would be a miracle if a train passed at exactly the right time every day. Also his school, the closest secondary, didn't let the animals escape until 3:20.

There was no sign of Teresa what's-her-name as he entered his corridor whiffing parfum de baked beans. He wondered if Cadogan would've noticed a meteorite smashing through the roof he worked on. Only if it put out his fag.

No more holes in the kitchen sink. He put the still-intact kettle on for a coffee and eyes constantly on lookout, walked into the living room.

If he was tidier, Form 8b's maths homework books would've been back in his briefcase. Then Luke Darlow wouldn't have a hole in his simultaneous equations all the way from the front cover to the back. No way could he give it back to him like that.

He'd have to give him a detention for not handing it in. Shame he'd already corrected it. He looked up at the extra ceiling hole, wondering what else it went through.

The state of the bedroom carpet gave him a clue as he splashed through it to the radiator. The meteorite, or whatever, ricocheted off the radiator without going straight through but enough to have a small jet peeing onto the carpet. He taped a wad of blutak and placed a bowl beneath the persistent rogue drips.

Monday

Alan Cooper was dismissive of every theory involving local origins of the projectiles: they wouldn't be fast enough, assorted sizes would result, rail timetables too erratic in practice, as were children.

"No, John. Use your maths. We've thought that it can't be bits of a satellite because they'd be burnt up and would come in one go, but satellites do things on a very regular basis. Take Meteosat for instance. It's the main weather satellite you see pictures from on the telly, although it does a lot more than scan the earth for visible light and infra-red. Anyway, the point is that there are sensors and transmitters programmed to activate very regularly indeed. I know one that switches on every two hundred seconds."

"So?"

"Just suppose there is a fragment of a dark asteroid near to it. It might have gas pockets inside or just be unstable and sensitive to a burst of electromagnetic radiation like a transmitter near by."

"So when Meteosat, which I remember is on longitude zero, like my house, sends a particular burst of data at the same time each day, a pocket of gas erupts sending a fragment of asteroid off. Its initial speed mightn't be much but most burns and ablates in the atmosphere until it's the size of a grape and slams into my house."

"You've got it!" said the excited Cooper.

"Rubbish."

"Or it could be an asteroid in a polar orbit that happens to pass near Meteosat at the same time each day and—"

"You're obsessed with Meteosat because you did research on it and I live on the Greenwich Meridian. If that satellite is responsible, the time it would take for incoming to reach my house would put it at least an hour, say fifteen degrees farther to the west. In the Atlantic."

"Ye of little faith," smiled Cooper. "You've been doing some work on it haven't you. But, there's a veritable ring of geosynchronous satellites over the equator so it could be one at fifteen degrees east doing it."

"So the Prime Meridian has nothing to do with it after all. And like I said, millions of people must live on it."

"But they don't," he said, ignoring Forrister's first comment. "About six hundred houses in the whole world and two hundred and ninety of those are here in London."

"I don't believe it," Forrister said.

"Go to the Geography room and get the big Times Atlas. You'll see how much sea the Prime Meridian is over and that once out of London it travels over almost uninhabited areas. By chance no French town is exactly on it, no Spanish, nothing in the Sahara or the rest of west Africa, just missing Accra in Ghana and then nothing in the rest of the south Atlantic to Antarctica and up the rear end of our planet over the Pacific Ocean."

"Well, even so it's not fair. Why should my house be hit? About six houses in the world get hit by a meteorite every year so the odds are about one in a hundred million that my house would be hit."

"For one thing you shouldn't take it personally." Cooper was laughing.

"It's not funny!"

"I'm not laughing at your predicament but at your irrational response to it. Listen; if another house was hit, anyone living there could say the same thing. *Why me*? But that's giving the meteorite decision-making power. Come on, John. Look at it this way: if it has to be a house on the Prime Meridian there's a one in six hundred chance it'd be yours."

"All this talk of chances and probabilities have given me an idea to pay for the damage," Forrister said, brightening up. "The insurance wouldn't pay for non-manmade impacts but a bookie might."

"Brilliant," Cooper said, "you should place a bet that your house would be hit by a meteorite tomorrow. You should get good odds; not the ones we've been throwing around. They wouldn't want to bankrupt themselves."

"True, but they might accept a £10 bet on a thousand to one against. I'll pop in on the way home."

"Make sure none of the kids spot you."

"No problem. I'm a maths teacher. Gambling is applied probability theory."

It wasn't funny anymore. John had come home to find another hole in the kitchen floor and ceiling, which had come from the bedroom upstairs. It had ploughed through his pillow, sending bits of yellow Kapok everywhere. It could've been his brains instead if he'd taken a day off ill.

He had to move. Perhaps Cooper would put him up until the meteorites stopped. Suppose they didn't stop? Or not until his house was reduced to rubble with a crowd to watch the daily impact bouncing back into the air.

So much for his inheritance. He couldn't sell it with this going on, he'd be sued for withholding vital information.

On top of that the bookies wouldn't accept his bet. They had to ring their chief actuary, who wanted to know if it had happened before and who would verify it was a true meteorite, which meant finding it in the cellar.

Tuesday2

Lulu's *Shout* didn't wake him on his digital alarm. He hadn't been able to get to sleep until four, but once zonked stayed deep. Something in his body clock stirred him around eight thirty, when his arm reached out to strangle the clock and bring it to his eyes. He expected it to be distorted by a meteorite but he'd only forgotten to set it.

He forced his legs to find the floor. They were slow but faster than his brain. The sight of the phone made his hand reach for it, shortly followed by a semblance of intelligence.

"Alan, it's me. I can't come in today. I'm going to the police and whoever else they suggest. It's doing my head in, and it would have done literally yesterday if I'd gone for a nap in the afternoon."

"Got your bed, eh, scary stuff. Why is the thought of being killed while asleep more disturbing than when you're awake?"

"What are you on about, Alan?"

"Sorry, John, look, briefing is about to start. What shall I tell Bentley; you're not feeling yourself? In which case old boy, who are you feeling?"

"Chance would be a fine thing. Just tell him I'm not well and I'll be in tomorrow."

"You know where I live if you want a safe house for the night."

The police were very comforting. They said nothing like it has happened before and so it couldn't be happening now. They'd send a constable round in a few days, once they'd all stopped laughing. The police were also helpful in that they'd notify the planning enforcement officer, just to make sure he wasn't making any unauthorised alterations.

He spent some time with an estate agent seeking advice on selling a house that's more of a site of scientific interest. The best advice was to come clean and put it to auction. There would be interest in purchasing it as a novelty; and he could expect around £40k, which was better than a smack in the face but not much.

He was keen to get back by three. Not to go in but to observe the roof. His preparations were to buy a digital video camera, a tripod and hoped-for permission from Teresa Czzzzzetc to film from her penthouse. He was wearing out his finger on her bell when he saw her coming out of his own house.

"Hi, Teresa!"

"Oh, it's you, Mr Forrister. Why are you at my door?"

"I wanted to ask a favour," he said, neatly distracted from asking her the same question.

"What favour is that. I'm very busy."

"In case a meteorite hits my house again today I'd like to film it from your window if that's okay with you?" He smiled encouragement.

"It would reverse the situation: you looking at your own house from my window, wouldn't it?" she said without the smile that should have accompanied such irony.

"Is that a yes?"

"I suppose so but give me five minutes to tidy my things."

When he was allowed in, he asked: "By the way, what were you doing in my house? The builders come back?"

"No, you got post delivered to my house by mistake, it wouldn't fit your letter box."

He had a good view of his roof. It was overcast and the tarpaulin flapped a little in the wind. He looked up at the cloud base.

3:13 came and although he stared and filmed, he realised he wasn't going to see a meteorite. If the cloud wasn't there he might've seen a glow from the ionised air around it and maybe from its friction glow but at a few miles up it would slow and cool too much to glow. It might still be hot, especially when boring through his house, but he was so unlikely to actually see it with the naked eye. Hopefully, his camera might pick it up with image enhancement.

3:14 His eyes ached, monitoring every shadow; eagerly watching the starlings, trying to see what scared them when they squawked off.

3:15 His ears tired of intensive listening, trying to distinguish a small meteorite impact from the melee of Chingford's finest screaming kids, tormented trains, reverberating Number 212 buses and suburban mayhem, as well as the *accidental* dropping of a mug of coffee from Ms Czeremchka's hands.

3:16 He looked at his watch and refocused quickly on his roof when he realised he might've missed it.

3:17 A car pulled up sharply by his house. He could just make out a beefy woman dragging a boy up to his door. The prisoner was Luke Darlow. The one he had put in detention. His mum must have found out he wasn't in school and collected her son promptly to have it out with him.

"Teresa, is it possible to hang around for a few more minutes?" He'd given up filming, now it was past the assumed hit time.

"No, I need to get ready to go out; and please don't ask to come up here again," she said, shutting herself in the bathroom. Forrister pulled a long face at the residual vibrations before returning for a last glance out of the window. The Darlow woman was still there beating his door with one fist with the other clutching what might be Luke's detention notification. He shuffled around for while in Teresa's hallway before overcoming cowardice to bluff Mrs Darlow. To his surprise, Alan Cooper, who'd arrived to see the day's hit, had sent her on her way.

Cooper was rubbing his hands. "Come on John, I've sent the Darlows packing; let's see today's damage."

"You're keener than usual to take a measure of my misfortune."

"You're becoming a scientific oddity and celebrity. My Canadian friend contacted NASA."

"Really?" Forrister never dreamt anything happening to him would make a pencil twitch in the teeth of a Houston Mission Control egg-head.

"They've set up a preliminary project team to look into it. One of them, a Eugene Borelli, is currently on secondment at the Jodrell Bank radio telescope and is coming down to see us."

"Us?" repeated Forrister.

"Apparently they suspected the Chinese –"

"The Chinese have been bombarding my house?"

"No. Not directly. They have lots of satellites up there and the Pentagon think they've developed a killer satellite that can knock out others. One of them is a remote sensing satellite called Ziyuan that they think is being used as target practice."

"Does the maths work out, you know, the fifteen degrees more to the east than the prime meridian and all that?" asked Forrister.

"We were wrong by twenty-three hours. For Meteosat, it takes longer than I thought; but there are so many, such as the Ziyuan series in polar orbits."

"Incredible,' Forrister said, shaking his head as he unlocked his door. "All right, stop shoving, Alan.'"

"There's another hole in the kitchen ceiling, but I can't see where it went," said Cooper, who stooped to scrutinise the floor.

"Perhaps supplication to the Gods will help," Forrister said.

"It would be a first. Ah, you're giving me a clue."

Above the table against ghastly yellow wallpaper, was a wooden crucifix. It had probably been there for a century, but only very recently acquired an angled hole right in the middle.

"I assume it is today's," Alan said.

"I don't look at it every day, but there's sawdust on the table, and it matches the line of the hole in the ceiling. Which means–"

"It should've gone through to the lounge," Alan said, joining in the race round the wall. The exit hole in the soft plasterboard wall led to another hole in the floor to the metal scrap in the cellar.

"It might still be warm, I'd like to find it this time," Alan said.

In the cellar, their scrambling only resulted in dirty fingernails. There were so many lumps of metal—nuts, bolts and fragments; most blackened or rusty and many were slightly magnetic. Cooper had a magnet and wasted over an hour testing lumps, looking for repulsion since only two magnets can repel each other. Iron meteorites tend to be slightly magnetic. But no luck.

Wednesday2

John was exasperated. What with the Chinese and the supernatural against him he might as well take up the estate agent's suggestion of an auction and accept a tenth of the house's value. On the other hand the value of a pile of Victorian bricks and century-old plain and coloured glass, copper and lead probably came to about twenty grand. Though they'd have to shift it quickly before the diurnal meteorite bombardment reduced it all to dust.

On his way home, he called in at Price & Gamble, the estate agent he'd seen previously.

"Oh it's you, Mr Forrister," said the secretary.

"You own the house of God, and want to sell it!" boomed Mr Gamble coming in from an inner office.

"What?"

"Young Kate here belongs to The New Church of The Cross, and hearing of a rumour about a crucifix today, remembered you."

"But–"

"It's true then? The hand of God actually went through a crucifix? And in your house?" she said.

"Well a meteorite, or something did, yes."

"Please, please, please take me to see it, please." She clutched his lapels. Forrister couldn't remember the last time an attractive brunette threw herself at him so enthusiastically, even if he was only proxy for his pile of bricks.

"I'll come along too," said Gamble, "I am responsible for my female staff when they go in the field."

'"Since when?" Kate said.

Forrister was swept up in the moment, and a while later followed the whole office into his house. They ran about finding all the old holes and photographed the crucifix so much he was sure it would ignite. He found the day's new hole, while they were making tea and emptying his biscuit tin. The hole in the soap was neat but its continuation through the bath was another repair job. At least the rest of its journey merely added to the holes in the lower floors.

"Do you have any pets, John?" asked the increasingly familiar Kate. "Only it must be a bit scary for them not knowing where and when to hide."

"I hadn't given much thought to it. No wonder I haven't seen Felix since last Monday," he said grimly.

"What! The poor thing. You mean she was–"

"I'm kidding, I don't have a cat. Or a dog."

When their digital cameras ran out of memory, Gamble sat Forrister down at his own kitchen table.

"I'm not really sure what's happening here, and I know you don't, Mr Forrister, but that hole in the crucifix could make a big difference to the value of your property."

"It could?"

"You do still want to sell, and at a price you can get another, safer dwelling?"

"Yes of course. But who in their right mind would want it?"

"The Church. It doesn't have a mind. It has faith and miracles. Mr Forrister, you are in a fortunate position."

Forrister was about to make a suitable response when he heard the doorbell. He was too slow and Kate answered it, bringing in a large black overcoat, which wasn't quite big enough for Eugene Borelli and his NASA intentions. Forrister, spasmodically speechless with awe, gave him the tour, including the basement. Borelli was keen to get up into the attic and was astonished no one had investigated it, even though the builders had done some repairs.

After the estate agents left, Borelli spent two hours examining and photographing each hole and damage, although was a bit annoyed that some patching up had been carried out.

"Well, I still live here you know."

"More fool you, buddy."

"I think you're ready to leave now."

"I didn't mean to offend. I would like to return and take your cellar apart. I haven't seen anything that definitely came from a satellite yet. Then some of those holes you know–" He was interrupted by Cooper, pushing at the door bell and bringing more people with him, sporting cameras.

"Oh, come on, Alan, I'm shoving people out of the house now, not letting them in. It's getting late."

"Ten minutes, John. Are you Borelli…" and the two scientists did the tour again with whoever the other people were. Sounded like press. Forrister had the sneaky feeling that Cooper was making money out of the situation. He'd have to tackle him for a cut.

His chance came twenty minutes later but Alan pre-empted him.

"I've learnt so much from that man. Apparently we're either looking for siderites, which are iron meteorites or the harder bits of satellites. Besides using magnetic properties—a failure as we know—the timing of impact might help. For instance, our solar day is twenty four hours but from the point of view of a star or asteroid the sidereal day is more relevant."

"And the sidereal day is–"

"Shorter than the ordinary or solar day. It's because the earth travels around the sun and so has to rotate a little more each day than would appear from a fixed star. What it means is that if the meteorites are hitting your house about four minutes less each day it's more likely to be meteorite than satellite in origin. We aren't absolutely sure each hits at spot-on three-fifteen, are we?" he said looking pleased with himself.

"Unless it's both," said a tired Forrister.

"What…oh yes, a satellite's transmission triggering bits off an asteroid. I forgot about that. Never mind. Look, I have another –"

"Good night, Alan. See you in the morning."

Thursday2

12:08 in the staff room; Forrister took a call from Mr Gamble.

"How does eight hundred and sixty-five thousand sound to you, Mr Forrister?"

"I couldn't possibly afford it."

"No, it's what you've been offered for your house, no strings, no chain, just a genuine big cheque. Minus our commission of course. Don't forget it has no central heating, double-glazing, no maintenance for nearly a century, so normally it would struggle to reach two-hundred thousand."

"Is this the freaky religious sect you mentioned?"

"There's nothing freaky about a suitcase full of money, Mr Forrister."

"Actually there is, but when could it happen?"

"If you agree now, come in to sign after work, borrow the school minibus to move out, and you can buy a deluxe Regency-mode air raid shelter tomorrow."

A flurried paperwork session followed, and Forrister stood in a daze with a bill of sale in his hand. He rushed round to his bank before they closed, and called in at Walthamstow Furniture Removals and Storage.

He called George Bentley at the school. He knew he'd still be there sorting out the next day's cover lessons. Although teachers were allowed time off for moving house it was usual to give notice, so he had to be more obsequious than he'd like. He almost skipped home. Home? He'd find a B&B for a couple of weeks until he found a more permanent residence. Maybe a flat in a very tall building only he'd have the ground floor or even the cellar, especially if it had a stone floor.

Once more, Alan Cooper was at his front door when the exuberant Forrister finally arrived home.

'Come in and have a serious drink, Alan, assuming my bottle of Grant's hasn't been trashed."

"Let me guess, you've had an offer for the house, and it's more than fifty quid."

"The God squad have bought it, and good riddance."

"Hey, will they still let the NASA guys in, and me?" asked Cooper.

Forrister laughed: "Maybe. What do you look like in a cassock?"

They crept in but couldn't find a fresh hole until Cooper went to the bathroom.

"Hey, John, your john's sprung a leak."

They looked at it. There was a neat hole in the plastic toilet seat cover but it looked as if a grenade had gone off in the bowl, with large cracks in the ceramic and a few pieces over the floor.

“There should be its continuation in the corridor downstairs,” said Cooper. They couldn’t find it. “Maybe it’s lodged in the wall or ceiling somewhere.”

“Let’s have that drink,” Forrister urged. “I can’t tell you what a relief it is to get out of here. I was mentally prepared to leave stoney broke, though at least I have a job. But now…”

Three hours later they smiled Alan’s way to the bus stop. John out for some fresh air.

As Cooper stepped onto the bus, Teresa disembarked.

“Hello there,” John said, “on your way home?”

“So?”

“You might be interested to know I’m moving.”

Friday2 Teresa

The smile continued to grow, completely out of control. It had been on her face throughout the night, in her dreams and now at the penthouse breakfast table.

The smile metamorphosed to rapid bursts of laughter as she stood with her steaming coffee and saw through the window the removals vehicle and men in overalls extracting the few sad bits of furniture worth keeping. Not bad—it had taken two weeks to rid herself of the peeping tom pervert. The whole point of moving to the penthouse in a politically Conservative London suburb was to put her private life away from such men.

Now look who had the power. She sat down again to finish her muesli and yoghurt, throwing a glance at the collection of her tools spilling out of the rucksack in the corner. A powerdrill, hole-borer, power-hammer, mini-vacuum cleaner and the keys. No point being the only girl and the only top grade in the NVQ engineering class at Wapping College unless you made use of it. As she took another mouthful, she ruminated on the pure luck of seeing the first and only meteorite hit on Forrister's house and the idea it gave her.

She stopped smiling to sip her coffee although she was still laughing inside. Her eyes opened wider as her ears picked up a noise. Before she could register what made it, the remains of her milky muesli splattered out in a corona as the bowl disintegrated. Even before she could take the mug from her lips she could see the hole where the bowl was and in her floor. It was 0814.

*****

ABOUT THE AUTHOR

***GEOFF NELDER** was a Geography and Maths teacher. He gained his MSc and Fellowship of the Royal Meteorological Society partly for research in weather satellites. In the research for this story he stayed at a Chingford hotel directly on the Prime Meridian and he spent a day walking that 0 degrees longitude from the northern to southern boundaries of London. Follow Geoff on Twitter:* @geoffnelder

Amazon Author Page/Geoff Nelder UK

Amazon Author Page/Geoff Nelder USA

Facebook/Geoff Nelder-AriaTrilogy

Wiki/Geoff Nelder-Aria

http://geoffnelder.com

THE AGENT

Alex Shaw

Carboneras, Spain.

Big Chris Cotton popped a breath mint into his mouth. He hated bad breath and in his line of business he'd encountered an awful lot of foul mouths. First impressions mattered to Cotton, and nothing gave a worse one than bad breath.

As the mint dissolved slowly he gazed out of the window at the dusty Spanish countryside gliding by. He was a city boy, first Chelmsford and then London, but now he was ready to retire disgracefully and move to the countryside. Well, semi-retire at least. In his industry only those who were dead took early retirement. Cotton wasn't dead, and didn't plan on being so for a long time yet. That was why he hired muscle like Vlad, who silently chauffeured him in the rented Opel Insignia. Not a patch on his Range Rover, which sat silently waiting for him back at Heathrow, but the best that the local Hertz office could muster. Cotton grunted. At least it was black and the tall Russian was doing a good job. It wasn't that Cotton couldn't fight—he'd had a reputation as one of the original 'Knife Men' back in the day—but just that he now saw it as beneath him.

He liked hiring 'Ivans' like Vlad. They were tough, followed orders, and knew when to keep their mouths shut. Cotton hadn't used local muscle since the fall of the Berlin Wall. First Poles, then Lithuanians, and now Russians had worked for him. They were happy with the wages he gave them, grateful to work in England, but most importantly were hard grafters. His business associates remained loyal to the local lads but Cotton had no time for dough-bellied Essex meatheads. The 'Ivans' knew what hard work was and they knew how to do it. Vlad was his new boy, he came from some small town near Moscow—Cotton couldn't remember where—and he'd worked for him for just over six months. Vlad was hired on the personal recommendation of his previous driver, who'd had to go back home to look after his elderly mum. Cotton had given him some 'wedge' to help out. He took care of his people.

The 'Ivans' were great workers and Vlad was no exception. He got Cotton out of a scrape with a couple of Glaswegian hard men a month back. The pair had waltzed into one of his clubs like they owned the place, not realising that he did. Vlad sent them packing back over Hadrian's Wall with their tartan skirts fluttering in the breeze. He didn't like the Scots—in fact he hated them. He hated a lot of people. The problem was they hated him back, but they also respected him. At least the older generation did, those who remembered the 'Knife Men'.

He crunched on the last bit of breath mint. Truth be told he wanted a break from it all. He needed to slow down a bit, to enjoy himself a little, especially now that his embarrassment of a wife was out of the way. He was well shot of her. He should have done it years ago but he'd become too caring. Yeah, that was it. He'd become soft, and what use was a soft hard-man? Still, he'd never been soft with his girls, the 'Olgas' who worked for his clubs. They loved it.

Cotton glanced at his large watch. He'd see the house and have a spot of lunch somewhere, probably tapas, before spending the night back in his hotel room sampling the 'local delicacies'. Life was good, and it was getting better. He let a lecherous grin split his pockmarked face.

Vlad slowed the Opel. Cotton's eyes narrowed as he peered through his darkened windows at the detached villa sitting behind a long low wall. "That it?"

"Yes Mr. Cotton." Vlad's English was perfect, but the accent Moscow Russian.

"Very Miami Vice," Cotton chuckled. He liked it. The old-school villains and lags bought places around the traditional tourist destinations of the Costa Blanca and the Costa del Sol, but Cotton had done his research and found that the province of Almeria, which sat squarely between the two, was less developed. He didn't want to leave Essex only to be confronted by orange tanned 'Easy Jetters' demanding pie, chips and sangria. Of course he didn't want to go native either, but there were limits. He regarded the villa through his tinted window. Gravitas was a word he'd heard that posh bloke from 'Grand Designs' use, and this place had it. Much more of it than the white boxes his 'business acquaintances' built for themselves.

"What's the name of the estate agent?"

"Terry French, Mr. Cotton."

"You spoke to him?"

"No, we exchanged emails."

"You can't beat a good phone call, except for a face to face." Cotton had people who did his e-stuff for him. It lessened his digital fingerprint and besides, he didn't really understand any of it. How could a photograph be sent from one computer to another? It was all too Star Trek in his opinion.

"Remind me of the price of this one?"

"One point four million Euros."

Cotton rolled his eyes. "Don't give me that funny money stuff, Vlad. What's it in pounds?"

"One moment." Vlad recalculated. "Just under one point one million pounds, Mr Cotton."

"Did you know Vlad me first gaff cost only twelve grand?"

"No Mr. Cotton. That is very cheap."

"Yeah. Sign of the times, son. It was me mum's old place, bought it off the council, done it up. Now look at me. Proper country gent."

Vlad manoeuvred the Opel through a large pair of ornate iron gates and parked in the house's impressive drive. He climbed out and opened Cotton's door.

"Ta." Cotton took a deep breath. "You smell that, Vlad? Proper sea air."

Vlad breathed in. "It is fresh."

"Wait with the car, this shouldn't take too long." Cotton put his Ray-Bans on.

"Yes Mr. Cotton."

Cotton's boat shoes squeaked on the Romanesque paving tiles as he made for the front door. He was annoyed that the estate agent wasn't outside waiting for him. Their first digression. He wouldn't tolerate any more. A giant palm tree stood on either side of the tall arch shaped front door, impassive sentries giving him the once over. Cotton placed his hand on the hefty looking brass knocker and banged the door. A moment later it was opened by a pretty brunette.

"You must be Mr. Cotton?"

"I must be." Cotton removed his shades as he looked her up and down. He didn't disguise that fact he liked what he saw. Business women 'did it' for him. Especially those who wore white linen suits.

She held out her hand. "I'm Terri French."

"I thought you were a man?"

Terri smiled. "In these heels?"

"No, I mean I thought I was meeting a man."

"It's an easy mistake to make."

Cotton nodded. "Never mind. Let's have a look around then?"

"Of course." Terri opened the door wider and Cotton stepped inside.

It took a moment for Cotton's eyes to adjust to the shadowy light filtering in through the windows. "It's dark."

"I'd say cosy."

Cotton inspected the dark tiled floor. He strode over to the wide staircase and tapped the bottom step with his foot. "Original?"

Terri tried not to frown. "Yes."

"Could it be changed? I mean, is this place listed or something?"

"I don't know if properties are listed in Spain. That's something I'd have to look into for you."

"Do so." Cotton crossed the hall and entered a stately room on the right. A tall window gave out onto the drive and a large fireplace took up most of one of the walls. "The room on the other side the same, is it?"

"Yes, this property is built around a central courtyard so you've a choice of four identical reception rooms. Is there a Mrs Cotton?"

"No." Cotton snapped before he regained his composure and his face softened. "Went our separate ways last year. Why do you ask?"

"I was going to say that you could have a wing each, you know, in case you wanted to do different things."

"That was why we parted, we wanted to do different things." Cotton had wanted to do his secretary and his wife hadn't.

Terri forced a smile. "Well, for a bachelor it's also a great property. Lots of room to entertain." Terri moved closer to him, he caught a whiff of her expensive perfume as she clicked on the light switch. "That chandelier really is quite something. You could have a lot of parties in here."

"I like to party." Cotton now smiled and looked into her eyes. They were the greenest he'd ever seen. "Do you?"

"I love to party." Terri returned his smile. "Who doesn't? Shall we see some more?"

Terri led him along the hall and across the courtyard. They entered another reception room, this one with views of the rear terrace, pool and the beach beyond.

"Now that I like." Cotton moved nearer to the window and squinted. He could just make out the faint outline of a yacht on the horizon. Through the open window he heard the bells of a distant church peal. "Don't believe in it meself. Do you?"

"I don't believe in heaven." Terri held his gaze. "I believe in hell. I believe that we must atone for our sins."

"That's a bit heavy, luv," Cotton chuckled. "I'm in deep 'doo doo' then."

Terri took a breath. "Shall we now go into the kitchen?"

"Why not, although I don't cook for meself so I wouldn't know what I was looking at. The missus used to deal with all that type of thing."

They turned back into the courtyard and then took a left into the kitchen. Large stone slabs lined the floor and the cooking utensils hung on hooks suspended from the ceiling. "Country chic they call it, but all very expensive."

"In a kitchen, that would be expensive tastes." Cotton chuckled. "Expensive tastes – get it?"

"I do," Terri smiled.

Cotton's eyes fell upon the hooks. "Now that's all a bit medieval, them things hanging like that." Cotton reached up and tugged at one of the hooks. "Doubt if it could hold anyone's weight."

"It's just for utensils. So what are your impressions so far, Mr Cotton?"

"You can call me Chris."

"So what are your impressions, Chris?" She beamed at him.

"I think you may well have yourself a sale here, luv. If of course there is room for negotiation?"

"I'm always open to negotiation." She crossed to the large American-style fridge, opened it and removed a bottle of champagne.

Cotton wagged his finger. "Now luv that is naughty. The bubbles in that make me do silly things. Did you put that in there, special?"

"I did."

"Then you are very naughty. And I'd be very rude not to have some."

Terri handed him the bottle, "Can you open it, I'm always afraid I'll shoot myself in the face with the cork."

"My pleasure." Cotton undid the foil, then loosened the wire cage before he expertly pushed the cork upwards. Terri produced two champagne flutes and placed them on the worktop. Cotton tilted the bottle with practiced precision, filling both glasses before he put the bottle down and handed a flute to Terri. "Cheers!"

"Here's to negotiations?" Terri said with a wink. They both drank. She downed hers in a single gulp. Cotton raised his eyebrows. "Sorry, I was thirsty."

He pointed with his glass. "I like a woman who isn't afraid to drink. Let me give you a top up?"

"Please." Terri's smiled widened. Cotton handed her the glass. She raised it to her mouth but her hand shook and she spilt the contents down her blouse, dowsing her cleavage in champagne.

Cotton made no effort to remove his eyes from her now see-through top. "I'm sorry."

"No, it was my fault. Let's go upstairs? You should have a look around, and I'll get a towel from the bathroom."

"Great idea." Cotton gestured with his chin for her to lead the way as he held his glass in one hand and the bottle of Bollinger in the other. He followed her out of the kitchen, along the hall, and up the stairs, all the time keeping his eyes fixed on her bum as is twitched beneath her tight, short skirt. He felt his loins stirring. "The more I see the more I like."

"It has some great views." Terri replied, seemingly oblivious to the innuendo.

They reached the landing and Terri pointed to a room on the right. "That's the master bedroom. There's a fantastic sea view. Why don't you have a look in there whilst I try to dry this?"

"Okay." Cotton walked away with a smile on his face. If he played his cards right he could be onto something here. Like the rest of the house, the walls of the bedroom where white and met the same terracotta tiled floor – not his style but he'd soon fix that. A four-poster bed touched the back wall. He sat on it and checked the springs. It would do for a quick one anyway. The doors to the balcony were open. He rose and stepped through them. Terri was right, the view was fantastic. Immediately below was the terrace, which gave out onto the pool, garden, and then the sandy beach. He refilled his champagne flute and placed the bottle on a patio table. He took a long pull, closed his eyes and let the breeze wash away the fatigue of travel and the stress of business.

"Do you fancy a quick dip?"

Cotton open his eyes and turned. Terri was standing in the doorway without her blouse. For a moment he was speechless as his gawped at her toned stomach and perfect breasts visible under her translucent white, lacy bra. She made no attempt to cover herself and raised her eyebrow coquettishly. "I did mean the pool, but…"

"Has anyone ever told you that you are absolutely stunning?"

"Yes, but not today."

He stepped forward, the bulge in his chinos now visible, and placed his left hand on her cheek. "I like the villa but you'll have to persuade me to take it."

"And how can I persuade you?" She leaned her head into his rough palm and then ran her right index finger down his neck until it touched the pendant hanging on his gold chain. Her eyes focussed on it, as though noticing the charm for the first time. "BC. What does that stand for?"

His hand dropped to her waist and he pulled her towards him, pressing himself against her. "I'll show you."

Terri stepped away. "Follow me, the master bathroom has a huge bath and I feel dirty."

Cotton grinned as they left the bedroom via the connecting door. She moved aside to let him enter. Cotton took a step, and then stopped, confused. "What's all this?"

"Your life, Christopher."

Cotton was unable to move for a moment as he registered the display before his eyes. The entire long, facing wall of the rectangular shaped bathroom was covered with photographs. It wasn't art, it wasn't decoration. It looked like the work of one of those stalkers or serial killers he'd seen on 'Dexter'. The snapshots were not in frames but affixed directly to the white tiles with bits of scotch tape. And the photographs were all of him His hand started to shake and he hungrily drained his champagne flute.

He took a hesitant step forward, then another. On the far left, past the large shower cubicle, a set of photographs showed him and his ex-wife. Some were sharp and in colour, others black and white, blurry and taken with a long lens. But what they all had in common was that they showed him dragging her by her arm, him raising his fist to strike her, or in a couple of cases, his fist connecting with her face. Cotton shook his head slowly.

He moved forward again, now within touching distance of the photographs, and followed them across the long wall with his thick fingertips like a blind man trying to find his way in an unfamiliar room.

"It's all there, in black and white." Terri paused, a smile formed on her face that he didn't see. "And in colour. We've got photographs of everything. The last few times you beat your wife, meetings with your associates, you receiving and checking shipments, and of course you taking care of business concerns. That grouping at the bottom left is worth a look. Remember Jimmy Gomez? That's you beating him to death."

Cotton spun, his face puce. He snapped his champagne flute in half and held up the jagged shaft. As he spoke, spittle flew from his mouth and his accent became decidedly more Essex. "I don't know who you really are lady or what you want but you ain't gonna get nothin from me. I'm gonna enjoy fuckin you and then I'm gonna fuck you up!"

"Baby Cock."

"What?" Cotton frowned.

"Isn't that what BC stands for?"

Cotton roared. He flung his left arm in anger against the wall and ripped off the nearest few photographs before rounding on her. "I'm gonna enjoy this, Terri. I ain't had a hate-fuck since I kicked the missis out!" Cotton lurched forward, left hand probing the air whilst his right held the broken glass. "It ain't a knife but it'll do the job!"

Although he was fast, and clearly skilled, Terri anticipated the first jab. She sidestepped the fist holding the improvised weapon and kicked him hard in the groin. "Ooh, BC."

Cotton coughed and doubled over. "Bitch!"

Terri kicked him again, this time her foot connected with the back of his right knee and he collapsed onto the floor. "Looks like I'm fuckin you up, BC."

Eyes wide, not quite believing his predicament, Cotton dragged himself across the tiles and back into the bedroom. The pain in his groin was like a red-hot weight pulling him to the floor. He reached the bed and used it to heave himself up, first to his haunches and then to his feet. In a mirror he saw her leaning against the doorframe with a grin on her face. "Now I enjoyed that," he said, taking a deep breath and trying to relax. "I like it when they fight back."

"Like Jimmy Gomez? Did you like it when he fought back?"

Cotton sneered. "Jimmy Gomez was a twenty-four-carat chutney!"

"But he fought back, he knocked one of your teeth out—I've got a photo."

"Is that what this is all about? Jimmy 'chutney' Gomez?"

"Yes."

Cotton took another deep breath and faced her. "Okay, you've had your fun. Now I really am gonna fuck you."

Terri changed her posture, her stance that of a trained fighter.

"I love it! I bloody love it!" Cotton roared as he charged at her. Terri tried to sidestep again but this time Cotton was wise to it and shot out his left elbow. It connected with her shoulder, just a glancing blow yet powerful enough to make Terri lose her footing and fall. She scrambled and rolled as Cotton tried to stop his own forward momentum. His right knee gave way and he landed face first, blood exploding from his mouth. He roared again in anger.

"Mr Cotton? Mr Cotton?" A voice called.

Cotton wiped his bloodied mouth with his hand. "In here Vlad, the master bedroom! You've had it now, fun time is over!"

Terri backed away, an amused expression on her face.

Cotton was on his knees and slowly getting to his feet when he saw the tall, dark haired Russian enter the room. "Vlad mate, hold her for me whilst I sort meself out?"

Vlad looked at Terri. He spoke, his accent now British Home Counties. "Any problems?"

She shook her head. "None that I couldn't handle, Aidan."

Cotton felt himself become slackjawed. His mouth opened and closed a couple of times before he managed to form any words. “Vlad … what the hell?”

Vlad stared the gangster squarely in the eyes. “My name isn’t Vlad. My name is Aidan Snow. I’m with the Foreign Office and I’m here, unofficially, to arrange your rendition to the Spanish authorities.”

“What you talking about?”

Terri spoke. “Christopher Cotton, my Director has requested that I collect you and transport you to Madrid.”

“Your Director?”

“Gerardo Gomez. You don’t know him, but he’s the head of the ‘Centro Nacional de Inteligencia’, that’s the Spanish Intelligence Agency to you, and he just happens to be the uncle of Jimmy Gomez. The innocent man you beat to death.”

Cotton felt his legs start to wobble. “Nah, this can’t be true. I ain’t havin’ it! D’ya here? I ain’t havin’ it! If you’ve got something on me prove it in court!”

“Who said you were going anywhere near a court?” Terri said.

“I got rights, there are laws. International laws to protect me!”

"You vanished whilst on holiday in Spain," Aidan Snow stated, "just one of the many British criminals to go missing in continental Europe each year."

Cotton looked at the man who now called himself Aidan before pointing at Terri. "What's your name? Your real name?"

"I could tell you, but then I'd have to kill you," Terri said flatly.

Cotton started to shake. He puffed his chest out and balled his fists. "You'll need an army to take me! A fuckin army!"

Snow cocked his head. He heard a distant yet recognisable sound, helicopter rotor blades. "She has one."

*****

ABOUT THE AUTHOR

ALEX SHAW *spent the second half of the 1990s in Kyiv, Ukraine, teaching Drama and running his own business consultancy before* *being head-hunted for a division of Siemens. The next few years saw him doing business for the company across the former USSR, the Middle East, and Africa. Alex is an active member of the ITW (The International Thriller Writers organisation) and the CWA (the Crime Writers Association).*

He is the author of the #1 International Kindle Bestselling ***'Aidan Snow SAS thrillers' Cold Blood, Cold Black, Cold East*** *(commercially published by Endeavour Press in English and Luzifer Verlag in German) and the new* ***Delta Force Vampire*** *series of books. His writing has been published in the thriller anthologies* ***Death Toll, Death Toll 2, Action Pulse Pounding Tales 2*** *and* ***Capital Crimes****.*

Alex, his wife and their two sons divide their time between homes in Kyiv, Ukraine and Worthing, England. Follow Alex on Twitter: @alexshawhetman or find him on Facebook.

SKULLY

C.A. Sanders

I can tell you what happened that day and why your Uncle Wallace is like that, but you won't believe me. He'll deny everything anyway. I don't know if he even remembers it, at least not the way I do. I don't blame him.

I was only nine, and Wallace was eleven. We were outside our building, playing Skully in the street. Skully's kind of like half hopscotch, half horseshoes, and—I don't know—half talking trash until you make someone cry. We chalked out a big square in front of the stoop, and then a bunch of little numbered boxes inside of it. In the center was the final box, and surrounding that, we drew a box marked with skulls. If you flick your cap in there, you're stuck until someone knocks you out. Nobody ever knocks you out.

So that day, it was five of us: Wallace, his best friend Vin, Vin's little half-brother Nando, and Sunil, my best friend back then. Your dad was probably playing basketball with the teenagers, or maybe working at Lampston's. He was so much older, he almost never played with us.

Like I said, Skully is all about trash talking, and your Uncle Wallace was the master. He could psyche anyone out. Usually, it was me.

"You went out of turn, Jimbo!" shouted Wallace. "Free kick, dumbass."

"Bu—but you just said it was my turn," I said.

"Yeah. Sucks, don't it." Vin laughed as Wallace—in slow motion for extra torment—kicked my poor skully piece into the sewer drain.

"You're an--" Well, I won't tell you what I said, but he deserved it. I worked so hard on that piece, fitting the Play-Doh in the cap just right, topping it with a penny for decoration. Yeah, I had spares in my pocket, but that was my favorite.

"And you're out of the game. Go burn your ass on the slide." He pointed to the large, metal slide in the sandbox playground across the street. Blinding light reflected from it. In the sun, those slides are like nuclear hot. Joe Marcone burned the skin off the back of his thighs two weeks before. Actually, the playground was pretty cool if you ignored the broken crack vials, and even they could be fun. They fit right into your GI Joe's kung fu grip.

I probably shouldn't have told you that. Your dad's gonna be pissed … I mean, upset.

Anyway, I sat on the stoop instead and watched the other guys play. Nando was really good, especially since he was only seven and had Vin constantly punching him in the arm. He moved from box to box with no problem. But like I said, your Uncle Wallace was the master. He didn't just score by getting his piece in the boxes, he knocked out other kids' pieces and moved ahead like that.

Yeah, I know it doesn't sound like him, but it's the truth.

So Wallace won again, no surprise. He scooped up the rolls of Smarties that we bet with and did his little victory dance, which was him basically stomping on everyone's piece and making fun of their mommas. We were going to play again, but we heard the Mister Softee song and ran down the block. You don't know the song, but Mister Softee's like the pied piper of ice cream trucks. I haven't lived in the city in a long time, but it never feels like summer without that song.

The yellow-haired kid was waiting when we came back.

You gotta understand, I never saw a kid with yellow hair before, except on TV. I mean, there were a couple of blond kids on the block, but this was yellow, like sunshine yellow. It was long too, like something you'd see in California. We just didn't do that in the Bronx. You'd get it caught in an elevator or something. Joe Marcone once got his book bag caught in one, and it was ugly.

He was sitting on the stoop, and I sat down next to him. "Hey, I'm Jimbo. You new here?"

"Yeah, we just moved in next door." He smiled and tugged at his Pac-Man T shirt. I decided that I liked the kid. You know how sometimes you just like someone when you meet them? Like how you know you're gonna be good friends? That's what it was like with this kid. Me, him, and Sunil, we were gonna be best friends forever.

We talked while the other kids played another round of Skully, another victory for Wallace, who jumped around and named himself "The Killa Dilla." The yellow-haired kid was funny, cracking jokes and spitting on the ground like a teenager. I even gave him the last part of my ice cream, the melty part that's always stuck in the bottom of the cone.

He reached into his pocket and pulled out Zartan, one of the best GI Joe toys ever. He held Zartan up to the sun, and the toy's face turned blue. How awesome is that? Sunil gave me a jealous look, and for a long moment I hated him. Why couldn't he just come over and be cool with us?

Wallace and Vin started arguing about who was gonna start the next game. Nando took his half-brother's side, but Vin slapped him away.

"Can I play with you?" the kid asked as he stood up. He brushed the hair from his eyes. His eyes were blue. I mean, really blue, like Cookie Monster blue. This was a freaky kid, but not bad. I wasn't weirded out or anything. He was different, but I was different too.

"We play for candy, kid," said Vin, puffing out his chest and wiping his ice cream-covered hand on his shirt. "You got?"

"Is this good," he answered. He reached into his pocket and procured a blue Ring Pop, the greatest flavor of them all.

"That's goin' right in my stash. I'm gonna wear that all day long," said Wallace. "You got a skully piece?"

The kid reached into his pocket and pulled out a Michelob cap stuffed with blue Play-Doh. "I'm not very good, so take it easy on me."

Wallace, Vin, and Nando laughed.

"What're you laughing at?" Vin said to Nando. Nando leapt away, keeping Vin from using Nando's hair to wipe his dirty hand.

"You go first, kid," said Vin. "Watch out for the drain. Your piece falls in, you're out." He laughed, "Get it?"

The new kid stood at the line and took a deep breath. A tumbleweed of cassette ribbon blew across the board. He tossed his piece. It sailed past the first box and rolled off the curb, stopping underneath a Yugo's front tire.

"Heh, you suck at this," said Wallace.

"I told you. We didn't play this in my old neighborhood."

The boys snickered and took turns throwing snaps at the boy and his momma. The kid wiped his eyes, and a stiff wind blew his hair across his face.

"Aw, look at him," said Vin. "He's gonna cry."

"I'm not … I'm just—"

"Crying," said Wallace.

"Stop, I'm …" the yellow-haired boy brushed the hair out of his eyes. His eyes weren't Cookie Monster blue like before. They were pale, like an empty sky. "I don't want to play for candy. That's stupid."

"You wanna play for money?" asked Vin, punctuating with a lick of his chocolate cone.

"How about," the yellow-haired boy looked Vin in the face, "if you win, I'll do whatever you say for a day, like a slave."

"You're an idiot, kid. I don't know if you noticed, but I'm a cold bastard," said Vin.

He didn't actually say "bastard," but you can guess.

"Let him do it," said Wallace. He looked at the yellow-haired kid. "What do you get when you win?"

"The same thing … but … but forever. Yeah, forever."

The older kids laughed at him, and he blushed. The wind swirled through the playground. I felt so bad. Wallace and Vin were gonna torture him, and he didn't even know it. I kinda wished it would rain and end the game. I thought about quitting and taking the kid and Sunil to the playground. I had two GI Joes in my pocket. We could play with Zartan and give them broken crack vials for grenades.

"Unless you're a chicken," the kid added, and I got a chill. "I dare ya."

"Whatever, fine. Let's play." Vin stepped forward and flicked his skully cap. He landed in the first box with no problem, then threw across the board and just missed the second.

Wallace rubbed his cap between his hands. "Now watch how the Killa Dilla does it." He tossed the cap, and moved with ease all the way to the fourth box. "Don't worry, kid. Even if I win, I'd rather have your Ring Pop. Jimbo's the only slave I need."

"Thanks, I guess," said the new kid. "You're much better at this than me. I hope you guys don't hold me to it. I'm an idiot."

Vin nudged his brother. "Nando, it's your turn."

"It is?"

"No it's not," said Wallace. "Nice try Vin, but you suck at the psyche out. It's Jimbo's turn," he looked at me. "Go already."

I knew what he was trying. He wanted to make me think that it wasn't my turn, so Sunil would go and get his piece kicked into the street. But I was paying attention this time and didn't bite.

I missed the first box and stepped back to the new kid. Sunil toed the line. Vin and Wallace kept shouting "Jinx" as he got ready, and each time he pulled the cap back.

"You don't think they'll really hold me to the bet, do you? I was just playing around. I didn't realize the game was so serious."

"Vin might."

"Why do you play with him then?"

"There's not much else to do. The older kids won't let us play basketball with them, and sitting in the apartment sucks. It's so small you can hardly move. Where'd you move from?"

He brushed his hair from his eyes. "The other side of the Bronx, but it doesn't matter. It sucks everywhere. Dad says the city's going to hell."

"Yeah, Mom says the same thing. She says I gotta get to college and never come back. She cries a lot. She says crying gets the sad out."

"It doesn't," he said. "Nothing does. I think it's my turn." The kid stepped into the street, by the old Yugo. He bent down to his piece, and easily flipped the cap into the first box. "That's one." He tossed to the second, and it landed in the center.

"You tricked us!" shouted Vin. "You're a freakin' ringer."

"Yeah, but it's ok. You said you're a cold bastard." The boy lined his shot at Vin's piece. A sharp flick sent his piece crashing into Vin's. The boys cheered as Vin's piece landed in the center box—the Skull.

"You're out. You have to do what I say now."

"Eat sh--"

The words froze in Vin's mouth, as the kid raised one hand. "Go sit on the stoop and pick your ass." The wind caught the boy's yellow hair and blew it back from his face. His eyes weren't blue anymore, but a greenish yellow, almost like a cat's. A flash later, they were blue. I thought it was the sun, and I'm still not sure. You know, memory's like that.

"Yeah, good idea." Vin dropped his ice cream and sat down. One hand went down the back of his pants.

The kid knelt down, and with hardly a touch, he knocked Nando's battered beer cap into the skull box. "That's for laughing at my friend. Go to the stoop." The wind rustled Nando's thick hair, and he sat next to his half-brother.

"The hell's going on?" Wallace said. "Vin, get off the stoop, and get your hand outta your ass." He grabbed Vin by the shoulder, but he wouldn't budge. "Kid, what the hell did you do?"

"I'm playing." The boy slid to his piece and knocked it into Wallace's at an impossible angle. The piece rolled on its side, skirting the skull, tracing the outline of the box until it fell just inside the corner, barely enough to make it count. "Give all your candy to Jimbo." Wallace reached into his pockets and pulled out two handfuls of Smarties and tried to put them in my hand. I let them fall to the pavement.

Now I was crying. It didn't take a lot to make me cry back then, but this was way beyond normal tears. I noticed that no adults had walked by or through the board since the kid showed up. No one even went into the building or came out. It was like the whole world was dead, except for the game and the now-cracked bits of candy.

Sunil grabbed my arm and tried to pull me away. Tears stained his face and shone. "We gotta run. Hurry"

"Yeah," and I stumbled after him.

The kid raised his hand again. "Wait, I thought we were gonna be friends. The bad kids won't bother you anymore. They'll do what I tell them too. If I say never make fun of you, they won't. If you want them to do your homework, or beat up a bully, they will. I can tell them that right now, if you want. We can even stop the game and take off the bet. I don't want you to be like them. I want friends."

"You're not my friend!" Sunil put up his fists like he wanted to fight.

"That's OK, Jimbo is." Another perfect shot, and Sunil was sitting on the stoop. "I guess it's just us to be best friends now. It's better this way. I don't think he ever liked me. Do you want to stop the game and play GI Joes?" He put his hand on my shoulder.

"They're like zombies. Why did you do that?"

"They're not zombies. They made a bet, and they lost. They shouldn't have bet what they couldn't stand to lose."

I wiped my nose on my arm, and it slicked my arm hair. "Put them back normal again. Can you do that, please?"

"If I tell them to be normal, they'll be mean again. I won't let them hurt you. Let's stop playing Skully. Let's play something else. We can go on the monkey bars or down to the bodega and get more candy."

So, ever get this feeling like you know something, and you have no idea how you know it? It's like, my brain was working on something inside without telling me, and it told me to try. I shook, but for once, I did it.

"Let's keep playing," I said. I couldn't believe that I said it, and I wondered if the kid was making me say it.

"Why? I don't want to beat you. I don't want to have to tell you to be my friend." He moved to his piece and gently tapped it. "See? My turn's over."

"Ok, let's change the bet then," I said. "If you win, I'll be your best friend forever."

"Forever?"

"And ever. But if I win, you gotta set them all free."

"Do you know how long forever is?" he asked.

"Yeah, a long time. Can we play?"

He smiled wide. "OK, but I'm not gonna take it easy on you cause you're my friend."

"Fine. It's my turn."

Now I said that no one ever knocked you out of the skull box, but that's just because no one wanted to risk it. If you try and fail, you're stuck and they'll never stop making fun of you. But Wallace's piece was right on the edge, and I was feeling lucky.

I took careful aim, cocked my middle finger with my thumb, and flicked a perfect shot, more perfect than any shot I've ever made. It struck his cap and sent it sliding out of the box, while mine went the other way, safely in open space.

Wallace jumped off the stoop and got right in the kid's face, screaming, cursing, and threatening to tear off the kid's head and do something awful to his neck. The kid took it all, unflinching, unafraid, even though Wallace was much bigger than him.

It was still my turn. I knelt down and cocked my finger again. I looked at Wallace, he looked at me. He'd done this a hundred times before. Usually I was the victim, but I learned.

Wallace grabbed the kid by the shoulder, distracting him for just a moment. I cursed, and stood back up. "Damn, I missed." I stuck the finger in my mouth, finishing the lie. "Scraped my finger. You go, kid."

"What? Oh." He moved to his piece and lined up to freeze Wallace again. "Wait, isn't it Wallace's turn?"

My heart jumped into my throat. "Nah ah. Neighborhood rule. If someone knocks you out of skulls, you still lose your next turn."

"I never heard of that."

"Yeah, but you said that you never played Skully in your old neighborhood."

"I dunno," he said. The wind began to pick up, and a few drops of rain fell.

"Come on, before the storm starts."

"The storm will start when I say it starts. My dad wants me to have friends."

"Just go," Wallace shouted, followed by a string of curses.

The yellow-haired kid turned red. "Fine. I liked you better when you didn't talk. I'll make sure you don't again." He knelt down and easily knocked Wallace's piece into the skull box.

Nothing happened.

The kid stared, growling like an animal. A heavy breeze swept down, blowing garbage across the board.

"You skipped Wallace's turn," I said. "Free kick."

Wallace danced forward, threw his leg back like a cartoon, and kicked the kid's piece into the gutter. "You're out, dumbass."

Vin, Nando, and Sunil all blinked their eyes and stood up. Vin stopped picking his butt. They crowded around us three.

The kid hung his head, and the long yellow locks fell over his face. The rain fell harder, making our T shirts stick to our skin. "You lied to me, Jimbo. I thought you were my friend. We were gonna be best friends."

"I'm sorry, but Skully isn't about flicking stupid caps. It's about lying."

"You don't want to be my friend. You never did."

I tried to tell him that I did, but Wallace stepped in front and pushed the kid. "Get out of here. We don't want you around."

The kid reached back and leapt at Wallace, socking him in the jaw. It didn't matter that Wallace was so much taller and older, the kid was strong. I swear I heard thunder when he hit him. Wallace went down in a heap and rolled onto the skull box.

"Fine! I didn't want to be your friend either!" The kid ran around the corner, and we could hear his wails even after he turned.

I helped Wallace up and asked if he was ok. He said he was, but he wasn't. His eyes were glassy, and he mumbled.

Yeah, that's why he still mumbles, and why he's always flicking bottle caps. He's still the Killa Dilla.

I saw the yellow-haired kid sometimes in the neighborhood. He never spoke to me or even looked at me. He was always followed by a string of slack-jawed kids as they walked off to the sandbox to play with GI Joes.

*****

ABOUT THE AUTHOR

C.A. Sanders *is an author, journalist, and teacher. His debut novel,* ***Song of Simon****, was published in 2013. His latest release is* ***The Watchmage of Old New York****, based on his popular serial of the same name.*

A life-long New Yorker, C.A. lives in the suburbs of NYC with a turtle that he has had since he was six years old. He is patiently waiting for MetroNorth service in his area.

C.A. is an unabashed geek and Dungeons & Dragons addict. He is also "the most dastardly Skully player to ever live." If you don't know what Skully is, he'll be happy to teach you...the hard way.

Visit C.A. Sanders at www.casanders.net or on Twitter @CraigASanders

THE 13TH SIGN

Jean Gill

Ophiuchus smote mightily and the beast quailed.

Ophiuchus smote mightily and the beast showed its teeth in desperate encouragement.

Ophiuchus smote mightily and the beast hid its head between its griffin feet, groaning in despair. Smiting was only one of the divine skills in which Ophiuchus was lacking. No ordinary beast, Sirius XXIV would have rather faced the concrete maze than serve a wannabe Zodiac Sign like Ophiuchus. Or so Sirius would have claimed before he was faced with the concrete maze; he then chose to go questing with Ophiuchus. To quote the sage Nowal; hypothetical choice is an opportunity to show the qualities you wish you had.

Having made a real choice, the real Sirius flopped one silvery ear over his eyes and tried to shut out an off-key heroic saga with the other two. Even fur-insulated ears allowed snatches of 'smite/fight/bite' to reach his beleaguered brain, 'plight/flight/trite' seemed more suitable. And why was 'dog-eared' descriptive of tattiness?

Sirius contemplated the hairy interior of one ear with appreciation. Perhaps he could use herbal hair-thickener to improve the sound-proofing. Ophiuchus had reached the chorus; 'winner... princess...'

'Dinner... tinned mess' mused Sirius, son of Sirius, grandson of Sirius to the fortieth generation of noble questing beast. As a morale booster, he imagined the concrete maze.

Shuffling uncomfortably on the rocks, Ophiuchus pulled the sacred scroll out of his pocket, somewhat the worse for wear from chewing-gum and crumbled beast biscuit. The thirteen tasks were written in drip-proof gothic, the curly tails embellished with gold spots. A few peacocks must be missing tail feathers to judge by the illuminated margins.

The new administrative assistant to the gods was implementing the principles of TQUM (Total Quality Universe Management) with a degree of over-enthusiasm—an honours degree—and her mission statement, 'Presentation is All', was the only part of the document which could be deciphered.

Perhaps Sirius could sniff out its meanings; why keep a questing beast and research yourself? He glanced at the lumpy rug which was technically lying by his side while maintaining that aura of distance perfected in a parallel universe by English aristocrats and Japanese bathers. Sirius would need a little time to recover from smitings of such magnificence, thought Ophiuchus smugly. They would both need time to recover from the Sending itself.

+

In the formalities of the Sending had been a short speech from Taurus, who emphasised the importance of practising the seven sacred skills, among which smiting certainly figured. Ophiuchus would need to successfully complete the quest in order to take up full status as a Zodiac Sign with his own dates. As Ophiuchus recalled events, there had been much clearing of bovine throat and the speech had gone something like, 'I am going to talk serious bull,' (pause and prolonged eye contact).

'Secrete the sacred scroll; saddle the seven skills; *souviens que* success scintillates.'

Ophiuchus had wiped the spit from his forehead as unobtrusively as possible, committed the wise words to memory and thanked his elder. The other Signs had been standing at a distance, heads bowed reverently out of range.

Only when Ophiuchus said, 'Goodbye everybody. Wish me luck,' in his small boy's voice, did the Signs look up, gather round him, and say, 'All the best, old man,' 'That's the ticket,' 'Chin up' and all the other adieus which generally accompany a man being sent to his death in the battlefield.

If only his parents had timed his conception so that he was one of the Zodiac constellations when Saucero noticed them and accidentally fixed the nonscience of astrology for Alltime. Instead, he had been born one hundred years later when no one seemed willing to acknowledge a thirteenth Sign. There was little Ophiuchus did not know about institutionalised numerism, expressed as bullying at an individual level.

He had been pinched by the Crab, shot by the Archer, had water poured over him regularly and what one Twin would do to him while the other was chattering distraction, had left him limping and lop-sided. All this would have been bearable, had it not been for the psychologically damaging justifications.

'You're odd, Ophiuchus,' a Twin told him.

'But so are one, three, seven ...'

The other Twin joined in. 'I think you missed out five but anyway the point is they're odd within a sequence, and the sequence stops at twelve.'

'But why does it stop at twelve.'

A Twin blocked further debate. 'Because it does.'

Ophiuchus might have remained frustrated but unscarred if the other Twin had not insisted, 'No, tell the boy the truth. He might as well hear it from us.'

'It might be better if he never knows but all right, if you insist. Twelve is the last good number. Thirteen is ... unnecessary.'

'It's not just unnecessary, Ophiuchus, it's bad! You're a bad number!'

'No, I'm not!'

'Yes, you are!'

'No, I'm not!'

'Yes, you are!'

'Prove it!' Ophiuchus demanded. Silence. 'See! You can't. I'm just like you, only I'm the thirteenth.'

Both Twins exploded into rapid-fire proof. 'Why are there twelve months then?'

'Why were there twelve apostles?'

'Why were there twelve pennies in a shilling? Or was it shillings in a pound. I forget now.'

'Because thirteen is BAD! '

Ophiuchus objected, 'But all these are arbitrary examples. There are more examples of ten of a something. And anyway it's culturally specific. And limited to a particular time.' (This is an approximation of Ophiuchus' response, based on lightyears of mentally rewriting his actual reply of 'Waaa, I hate you').

'Huh! Next he'll be saying that the Chaldean use of the abacus was limited to a particular race at a particular point in history!'

'Yes?'

'No hope, none at all. Let me put this simply Ophiuchus. You would be the thirteenth Zodiac Sign. Thirteen is unlucky. We can't have people born under an unlucky Zodiac Sign. And you'd have Christmas in your house ... it just doesn't sound right Christmas in the house of Ophiuchus ... and more importantly Capricorn would not like it.'

'He would really not like it...'

'It's for your own good...'

'Why not talk to Dai Monde about going into the family business?'

Once his father was mentioned, Ophiuchus knew he had lost. Dai Monde, token Welsh star with international aspirations ('I'm going to put the Monde in mondiale') was not an asset in his son's eyes. Dai's token job was the creation of a universal systems analyst, who had solved the twin problems of whether a tree exists (or in this case an object in space) when there is no one to hear it fall; and of regulating spaced-out planets, with a satisfyingly complex system of tokens.

Each constellation received a token proof of its existence and in return provided the token employee with insurance documentation in case of deep space collision. Prior to the token system, a particularly enjoyable spaced-out party had left so much cosmic debris that the question of liability had been raised in the highest quadrants (where much of the debris had gathered, in accordance with Space Law 7 *The more room, the more muck in one comer* and Space Law 12 *The muck stops here).* Yellow giants had become orange-yellow giants overnight, bending relativity one step beyond.

The systems analyst had responded with the light of speed to the inter-galactic crisis, mainly to divert attention from his name at the bottom of the party invitations. His assistant had said to him, sneering, 'What do you suggest, another token system?' and the rest was history. Except the part that was the assistant's story and she is still pursuing the longest suit in legal history, for sexual discrimination and misrepresentation of a casual word.

Dai had found his metier mondiale and it was only Time which stood between him and his Destiny, the token female who orbited contrariwise round her allotted galaxies. It was written in the Stars that they should meet; Virgo, who had a nasty sense of humour, had sprinkled party dust into the Milky Way spelling out 'Dai for me token'. The stars had brooded long over the ambiguity of this message, foreseeing murder or at least mayhem, but Dai had been unimpeded by any knowledge of punctuation or conventional lay-out and read it straight away as 'Dai for me', by Token. As there was only one token woman, he plotted a collision course for his unseen partner, made the necessary token gesture and they never looked back (only one of their more irritating habits).

Ophiuchus had been much loved by his token parents but he felt that certain aspects of his childhood had left him even more vulnerable to the bullying on the Zodiac circuit. Remarks on his parents' low points of origin were difficult to dismiss when his mother appeared, one breast neatly uncovered by cross-over lacings, or when his father discussed in a loud, slightly tipsy tone, how token registration could be recorded on a database. Ophiuchus regarded their daily rounds with contempt and set his eyes on the stars, determined to see his heavenly body up in lights one day.

From the start, Ophiuchus had known that his place was in the Zodiac, the first rank of constellations. Reaching for the stars was one thing; putting up with their back-biting was something completely and painfully different. It had taken several centuries before Ophiuchus had pulled off the political coup which had forced a Board Meeting. He had waited until the others were off-guard, recovering after an unpleasant misjudgement by the Sun and confusing astronomers with comet-like tails of apres-soleil. On a night when the ether below looked clear, he had power-packed every flasher in his system, drawing extra energy from a complex little particle system he had devised and then activated with tokens. By the time Capricorn had kicked him powerless it was too late.

He had been observed and recorded by Umth astronomers and the Signs had to satisfy Space Law I *Anything planet- dweller oids (humanoid or other) observe has to fit the development of oid explanation.* This was a particularly obscure law which fundamentalists considered to mean that the stars should behave according to absolute scientific principles. Luckily the only two existential fundamentalists lived in a remote corner of a quiet galaxy where they replaced the pleasures of sex with those of well-crafted wooden furniture.

Most stars believed that you could fool all of the people all of the time, if only you worked at it a little. Curving and bending the absolute had become second nature, a mere question of relativity. However, of all the absolute Laws, political expediency remained the highest, and an emergency Board Meeting took place in secrecy behind an eclipsed planet. Ophiuchus had exposed himself as a flasher to innumerable astronomers and as Nowal says, 'If you can't count them, you can't shoot their kneecaps.'

The debate raged for thirteen hours, which drove three astronomers to madness from the impossible absence of Zodiac constellations. A fourth was pronounced insane anyway to avoid contemplating the possible accuracy of his observations. At the end of the day (as Ophiuchus liked to call thirteen hours) verdict was passed. Ophiuchus had won! All he had to do was complete the necessary initiation ritual and be welcomed onto the team.

His Mum and Dad had sighed, wished him luck and re-arranged his bedroom as a study before he'd even packed his adventurer's rucksack. Encouraged by an offer of a belt glittering with tokens, and by the Twins standing on his head, Orion had presented Ophiuchus with one of his puppies, a young Sirius ready to cut his teeth on a quest and on almost any flesh near him. So here was Ophiuchus, fallen to Umth and puzzling once more over the sacred scroll with his adoring beast at his side.

+

'He's puzzling once more over the sacred scroll with his adoring beast at his side,' Aquarius informed the others, passing his hands three times over the surface of the water in his jar. To the untrained eye, the ripples suggested three sheep jumping a gate but Aquarius' affinity with water was unique. Affinity with wine was more common among the Signs.

'Adoring? I thought we had to force the beast to go.'

'Poetic license. How else would we get heroic sagas in the first place?'

'Why do you do that stuff with the hands. Does it help you see?'

'How can shuffling his hands help his eyesight?'

'No, I mean SEE as in being a SEER.'

'Does that rhyme with leer? Where's Virgo gone?'

'I pass my hands over the water to purify the vision.'

'Of course, standard Pass-over.'

'Standard push-over, more like.'

'Speaking of passing water, have you heard the one about...'

'Shut up, you old goat.'

'QUIET!' bellowed Taurus. 'Let's ruminate over the plan, the machinations, the conspiratorial plot regarding Of the Puke Cuss.' (or that is how it sounded to the Signs who were now quiet, heads down and out of range— 'conspiratorial plot' had been far-reaching).

'He'll heeeeeeear you,' worried Aries, who tended to bleat elongated vowel sounds when stressed; especially when the vowel sounds were also stressed.

'This is virtual reality, you sheep,' rebuked a Twin with the ready wit of a bird's second syllable. 'Of course he can't hear us.'

'Ooooooooh.'

'Any chance he'll complete the tasks?' asked Virgo in the sort of husky voice which raised more than a man's spirits. It was always difficult to remember what she'd actually said as the audial senses tended to re-script it as 'Come on big boy,' or 'Here I am,' or 'Anything you like.' Any relationship between Virgo and her name was purely historical, adding piquancy where none was needed. In theory, she was fully clothed, which was even more distracting than when she was naked. Diaphanous silks sculpted her curves with rainbows, undulating like an athletic lover.

The Twins cleared their throats and the Water Carrier hastily poured water on anyone whose eyes looked glazed.

'You must be joking!' was the only response to the actual question. 'Let's make sure.' Sagittarius stroked the curls of his beard, forgetting the effect on Planet Erth of his most casual gesture. The Sea of Japan promptly imitated the precise curls of the beard and the resulting regular curves, fine brushed in black on bright blue background, were the making of artist Pan so Kawasaki.

Sagittarius pulled an arrow out of his quiver and passed it to Virgo. Her eyes on him throughout, she stroked it from shaft to tip. The other Signs carefully tucked their tongues back in their mouths and noted, without surprise, that Arrow had come to life.

'I get it,' announced the Twins with glee, 'a companion Sending.' They too touched the arrow, tweaking its tail.

The other Signs joined in. Only Libra, Leo and Taurus refrained from adding a touch of malice to the creature. The hazy outline of a four-footed dog-like creature, with drooling maw and shaggy coat formed around the arrow.

Sagittarius touched its head and it cowered at his feet. 'Questing beast,' he proclaimed and the outline flickered with black flames. Satisfied, Sagittarius returned Arrow to its former shape, though it still glittered with life-force even when nocked in the great bow. 'Fly and find and fail the Quester,' intoned Sagittarius, invoking the various magic powers of alliteration, ambiguity and three. It was no secret that he aspired to the role of leader but he had not yet gained Taurus' skill in multi-lingual insertions, nor his spitting range.

'Do you think we should have named the Quester?' asked Virgo. Capricorn fainted with lust while beaming Signs thought she had said, 'Yes, oh yes, yes …'

+

Still out of breath, Oni sat cross-legged, concealing the Scroll with the long black hair which was her pride. Whenever possible, she sat like this, tucking her feet out of sight and allowing the swathes of black satin to catch the light, hoping that someone might be captivated by what they saw. No chance in this village! From birth the nick-name 'Big feet' had been awarded her, and in a community which prized dainty feet above all else in its women, she had been doomed to watch more fortunate girls blossom in praise and love. Now, she wouldn't have it any different. As a servant she hovered invisibly, listening to the Elders' conversations about government and politics, considered too ugly to be worth noticing.

She also fetched and carried for the women's pre-marriage parties, always listening and learning, until she knew more than anyone in the village of both women's and men's matters. 'Yin and yang' she whispered. And now she had gained the Elder's Task Scroll from her greedy brother, who'd swopped his chance at being a village Elder for an extra bowl of rice and some sugared crickets. He'd not wanted to try the tasks in the first place, not being gifted with either energy or intellect, but he was spiteful enough to reveal Oni's secret, so she must leave as soon as possible.

Her kerchief knotted firmly to a stick in ritual fashion, Oni bent to take one last drink from the pool. When she saw the second face reflected in the clear water, she thought that the Elders were already pursuing her with magic to drive her mad. She turned to face her enemy and found an odd-shaped creature, the size of a large dog, watching her with impossibly yellow, flickering eyes. Its coat was long and burnished, covering a body that seemed to have gone without food for too long. Oni knew how that felt.

'You poor love,' she said reaching out to fondle the bony head. The creature blinked but showed no sign of aggression. She unknotted the kerchief and broke off a piece of rice-cake, giving it to the animal, which devoured the morsel in one gulp. 'I can't give you more now,' she said. 'Try begging in the village.'

With determination, Oni tied up her pack once more; if it were not a pre-requisite of questing, no one in their right mind would go about with bundles on sticks, she thought grimly. A whine and pressure against her side alerted her to the continued presence of the hairy beast.

'Shoo,' she said, then felt immediately guilty as the animal's entire body shrunk in hunch-shouldered misery.

'Oh very well,' she said, 'but I wasn't planning on taking a pet with me!'

The shoulders immediately lifted, the gait brightened to a steady lope and Oni was rewarded with a stinging thwack across her thigh from a massive tail. 'Ow!' She stepped sideways quickly. 'There's some things you'll have to learn!' She regarded the offending tail, now brandished high, and forked. 'You need a name.' She looked again at its tail. 'I'll call you Arrow. That tail is just like an arrow-head.' The beast swung its great tail in approval and fell in beside her, padding across the reddening sands towards a horizon of ever more dunes.

+

The girl slept, wrapped up in her cloak, heedless of the cold, calculating stars above. Not so Arrow, whose powers drew strength from the sparkling Signs. He pawed the sand in grooves until dust motes formed in the starlight, shaping the one he sought. Crafted to be the Quester's doom, he yet had many choices as to how he achieved Oni's failure. In the swirling dust, he saw his hero, the Questing beast of Legend, Sirius, and the pathetic constellation who accompanied this immortal dog.

Brimming with the powers given him by the Signs, Arrow whispered his own spells, enmeshing two questers and two companions. There would indeed be a thirteenth sign, outshining all the rest. He would be avenged for all those years he'd spent in a quiver, less than archer. He would show how arch he could be and Sagittarius would regret underestimating his weapon.

Once Arrow had gained Sirius' trust, all the two of them had to do was carry out the thirteen impossible tasks and dispose of Ophiuchus and Oni. A token love affair should do the trick.

Blowing the dust back gently into a soft pillow, Arrow curled up against Oni, radiating warmth. He would need her until the tasks were completed.

*****

ABOUT THE AUTHOR

JEAN GILL *is a Welsh writer and photographer living in the south of France with a big white dog, a scruffy black dog, a Nikon D750 and a man. Her claim to fame is that she was the first woman to be a secondary Head Teacher in Carmarthenshire. She has* *published 18 books, and is mother or stepmother to five children so life was hectic. Sign up here for Jean's Newsletter to get her book* ***One Sixth of a Gill*** *(shortlisted for The Wishing Shelf Awards) FREE.*

www.jeangill.com

THE BURGLAR

Glen Barrera

The body rippled, and at the same time a sound emitted through the side of its mouth not unlike the sputtering of a motorbike muffled by distance.

It was alive then, and for the first time in what seemed a long while Harold Aly allowed himself what he felt was a full breath. The sweat flowed freely from his 250-lb frame, causing him to change his grip frequently, and only now, with the animal's movement, did he feel the cooling touch of the night wind.

He relaxed his body slightly, and then executed an incremental roll that might relieve the pressure on his hip. He was grateful for the September breeze, for it also brought the freshness of mown grass that if only for a moment brought a reprieve from the strong smell of animal, and, if it wasn't an illusion, blood. For the next few minutes he blew and spit with a combination of lips and tongue in an effort to dislodge the fur that had settled in his mouth, only to find his mouth still seeming full, as if the fur had outrageously taken root. With a bitter sigh, more at his indecision rather and his disposition, he waited and tried to gather his strength. It would probably start all over again in a few minutes, and he wanted his body as fresh as possible.

Two days before, the plan called for simplicity (the truth being that his economic situation and inexperience hadn't permitted a range of choice). The decision to burglarize had been reached, the house had been targeted, dark clothes from his closet and dresser were picked and hidden, and a long screwdriver from a set of five was selected from the garage. His only capital investment had been a pair of high-top, black, Blue Star/All Star sneakers purchased, somewhat reluctantly, with money taken from Carol's purse over a period of time—$55.95 that would have collected toward the purchase of an upgraded computer game system if all this hadn't come about.

It didn't seem a big deal now, almost too silly to contemplate, but then the question of whether to spend the money had been a major consideration. He already had a pair of black work shoes and dark socks that would allow him the concealment he required, but more important, and certainly childish in retrospect, he had an overwhelming need to save for that game system. He had wrestled with the dilemma most of Sunday night before reaching the conclusion that: 1) he would feel faster and more professional with new sneakers, and, 2) you have to spend money to make money. Harold believed that even if it wasn't the right decision, it would be the mature decision.

He still had the feeling, spitting fur notwithstanding, that the decision to burglarize also stemmed from mature thought, if you disregarded convention for a moment and focused on the purely mathematical notion of a straight line being the shortest distance between two points. If money and the need for money were construed as those points, the shortest distance would eliminate the propriety of work, or at least minimize the work required. Doctors, for one, were well versed in the principle and utilized it quite well. Some, like Carol's foot doctor – two minutes and a twist – were more than superb in their sense of application. However, if you didn't have the degree, or connections, a person was forced toward alternatives. From that standpoint then, mathematically and without the education, a fast burglary wasn't such a bad idea if you kept it simple and nobody got hurt. Besides, he had concluded, there were no options left.

It had been a year and a half since he had last worked, and only two weeks before his unemployment benefits ran out. Though Hopstead Tool kept insisting they would call him back any day, there was as much chance of that happening as a Happy

Hour in hell; and that's exactly what he told Ms. Odell in personnel. She was likely moving him down in the call-back-to-work list for what she called his "huffy" attitude, but that was something he could live with. If he wanted, he told himself, he could get a job with another company – just like that! Being very good at tool-and-die, in another couple of years he would have made foreman, assuming old man Hopstead retired by then. For now though, hell, he wasn't sure he wanted to go back to work for anyone. After a year and a half of not working, Harold had become quite comfortable with the idea.

It was habitual now for him to get up at 9:35, brush his teeth, wash quickly, wet down his errant hair, eat corn flakes, and then turn on Dr. Oz (he and Carol didn't have children so there were no examples to set). It was educational TV. In a small way, Harold felt like he was improving himself day to day. Later, he would take a long walk with the dog, sleep for an hour, eat leftovers from the pot, drink milk from the carton, make the bed and play computer battle games before Carol arrived home at six-fifteen. It was a simple yet satisfying day. The prospect of leaving all that for a full time job that would allow him retirement after 30 years, at a tremendous cut in income, was certainly an indignity to the mathematics involved.

Part-time wouldn't be bad, but there was little that interested him. When he checked last week, the best bet was pizza delivery. And that only because he might finagle free pizza.

"I've got my pride," he had explained to Carol the week before. "That's why I don't take anything that just happens to come along."

They'd been sitting at the kitchen table drinking morning coffee. It was Carol's day off. Dr. Oz would have to wait until the following day. Harold wore his frayed "house" jeans and a tee shirt. The gap between the two displayed a bulge of flesh and the dark hair of his stomach. Carol was still in her pink housecoat, her hair dishevelled. Even so, she was a pretty woman. Friends wondered what attracted her to him in the first place. Not that he was ugly for his thirty-five years—it was because he was so big, he guessed, or at least liked to believe. And because he was big he got into fights while growing up, and fights leave scars and broken noses, and lopsided ears. But they were a good combination. What Carol lacked in size was more than made up for in her mental proficiency. In other words, she could bend him, big as he was, with words. The fact that they came from such a sweet-looking, librarian-ish girl was all the more remarkable.

She had countered his remark that day with, "Your pride is worth spit on spinach, Harold. It doesn't add value to the meal any more than you do to this house. And if you don't start bringing in some money, you'd better start looking for someone else to support you."

So, there it was in a soft even tempo—and she hardly looked up from the morning newspaper. It was her style. She was good at it. He stood, kissed the top of her dark hair, and retired to the TV room where he began working on the plan that had initiated while walking his dog.

In truth, the phrase—the shortest distance between two points is a straight line—came first. It occurred to him a few weeks before during a typical two-hour wait at Unemployment Services as he contemplated the varied angles and complex curves that often interrupted the mathematical rule. Harold drew out the concept on the back of his Job Services envelope, using "money" and "the need for money" as his two points. It wasn't until he took a walk that day with his Spaniel that the concept found a plan.

It was an old house, in an old section of town. Victorian as far as he could tell, it was painted white and sitting on a corner lot surrounded by a tall, black wrought iron fence speckled with bird droppings. He peered through the bars and noticed an old woman, in her seventies at the least, bending slowly over a flowerbed. She was a heavy woman with a faded blue skirt that reached to her ankles, giving the impression, when fully turned and bent, of a tent. Every so often she would slowly straighten her frame, position a bra strap, and toss more weeds to the grass. Initially, the scene suggested nothing more than fall flowers and saggy breasts, but as he walked farther he began to see the house and woman in an expanded dimension. Ideas fell one upon another with machine-like regularity: to live there she had to be wealthy; the old house would have points of entry that wouldn't be difficult to overcome; she was old and her hearing would be faulty; and obviously, her reactions were slow. It was a strange transition of thought, he reflected, and had built with such astonishing rapidity that it was only a matter of seconds before a plan composed itself in his mind. It coupled nicely with the shortest distance theory.

Naturally, he tried to disregard the notion. After all, he wasn't a criminal. And while the principle was sound, there were certain moral issues at stake. Besides, what the hell would he do with the treasures he might bring from the house? Who would buy them? His mind, churning and on overdrive, spat out the answer: George.

Sure, George would buy anything he might resell at a higher price. He didn't exactly live on the legal side of life, but hadn't been convicted yet. Damn, those moral issues again. George (real name, Guido) didn't have a real job, drove a Caddy, lived in a big house just outside the city limits, and went to Europe every year—a study in mathematical principle, straight line.

But maybe Harold was splitting hairs, morally speaking. George was a decent guy. Didn't he recently buy three windows for the church? Hum, moral issues vs. mathematical principles…

Even at that point he wasn't convinced. It wasn't until the spit-on-spinach conversation that he was sure of it. It made up his mind.

He was startled to the present by the twitch of the dog's ear. Harold instinctively tightened the muscles on his arms and legs, already strained from the tension, like rubber bands at the point of snap. He wasn't sure because of the darkness, but from the weight, fur, and bulk of the dog, he guessed it to be either a Doberman or Rottweiler, possibly a combo. "Easy boy," he whispered.

The back legs of the dog did a sudden kick-up into the back of his own legs that had been wrapped around the animal. The pain, as the claws tore into calves already burning from the initial attack, was agonizing. The dog was extremely strong and within ten seconds it had clawed its way from Harold's confining legs, twisting to gain purchase on the ground. He tightened the pressure on its neck, aware that at any moment the dog could wrench free should either of his hands slip. With his left leg, he swung under the leg of the dog, tripping it to the ground once again. He covered it quickly with his other leg. His greatest advantage was the collar of heavy leather with the buckle and tag between his arm and the dog's throat. Using that thickness, he could apply enough pressure to hamper the dog's breathing. At the present, all he wanted was control. He added pressure. Like the first and second time, the dog began wheezing a high pitched, jagged sound, much like a tea pot at the instant of boil. This was followed by slowness, the relaxation of muscles, and the gradual cessation of movement as the animal reduced to a series of slight shudders. Harold rested his head against the dog, letting fur absorb his tears.

It had been a beautiful night for devious schemes, with the stars and moon tucked beneath a layer of lofty clouds, leaving a rich darkness to screen his movements. It was pure excitement when he left home at 1:30 a.m. Carol had been asleep when he put on his dark pants, long-sleeve sweatshirt, and Blue Star/All Stars with their once white strip at the bottom, now darkened with three coats of shoe polish. She wouldn't miss him. The sleeping pills she took typically put her out for the night. The Victorian was six blocks away, in the older section of town, where big rambling houses were once the rule. It used to be a nice, quiet neighborhood. That is, until Hopstead and a few other corporations moved in and began buying up the surrounding land. They then widened streets, built quickie subdivisions of cheaper housing, and brought in fast food joints, the only redeeming factor Harold could find in the name of progress. By car, even circling the block around the house, it took only four minutes for the trip. He parked down the street, far enough not to be noticed, yet close enough so he wouldn't have far to carry the goods he brought out. His plan was to go for the silver, small antiques, and money, if he could find it. Actually, he would settle for anything that might be of value.

Silently, he had slipped the latch on the gate and had just rounded the yard on the way to the rear windows, screwdriver in hand, when the dog attacked through the darkness. His arm automatically rose to cover his face, letting slip the screwdriver, which took flight to some distant point of grass. A second later he felt the pressure of teeth biting into his arm. From that time he couldn't recall all the twisting and grappling that brought the dog to its current position within his arms and legs, both of them taking labored breaths. He did know, right from the get-go, that from this position he could maintain some control by exerting pressure on the dog's throat. And as long as he had control, he had time to think.

The thoughts had been disjointed at first, but as he eased from panic everything assumed a sharper focus. Physically, he seemed all right. There was a throbbing in his arm from the bite, and the backs of his legs were stinging from where the dog's claws had driven into the skin. The blood oozed, but he didn't think it serious. His position on the ground was quite uncomfortable, teased now by moisture from the grass soaking through his sweatshirt and leaving a clammy, viscous residue as it combined with perspiration against his skin. Overall and considering, he felt pretty good. It was his mental condition, however, that concerned him. Why didn't he kill the dog?

He vaguely believed it might have something to do with crossing some invisible line along the shortest distance separating a real burglar (serious, professional, and ruthless in pursuit of his quest), from a burglar (amateurish, just supplementing income, wouldn't harm anyone). It was a difference that made what he was doing kind of a Robin Hood venture rather than an out-and-out crime. To kill a dog protecting the property, and then rob the house, would be crossing the line to a point that might not justify the means. It was the same line social drinkers tripped over on their way to drunkenness, or marijuana smokers tripped over on their way to harder drugs. It was a subtle difference, just a slight tip of the scale that could make something once harmless, wrong.

And it had been lurking within his straight-line theory all along. It frightened him to think how close he was to stumbling.

The problem was that no matter which way he went, the dog was sure to go. If he tried to leave the yard empty handed, with remorse and a promise to never attempt anything like this again, the dog would tear him apart before he reached the gate. He knew about dogs, and even in a weakened condition they would respond to instinct as though nothing were wrong. But then, killing the dog and robbing the house, would be no different than killing the dog and walking away. He called for help in a voice just loud enough so that no one would hear.

A guess at the time put it roughly around 2:30. He'd been inching on his side toward the gate with the dog cradled tightly in his arms and legs. The back of his sweatshirt had crept up his back leaving an area of bare skin shuffling against the grass, causing an itch of tortuous dimensions. Bugs had invaded his underwear. The worst moment came when a car passed throwing its headlight beam across his body as it turned the corner. He buried his head into the dog's fur, gasping as he realized what someone might think if he and the dog were seen in a position that could be construed, even remotely, as unholy. Oh God! Who'd believe him? No question, his life would be over.

He was close to panic in his rush to leave. Options turned over in his mind until only one was left: the shortest distance theory. He would simply drop the dog when he reached the gate, stand, and take whatever punishment the animal could provide in the short space of time it would take to make his escape. Twice the doge had nipped at his face as they crawled, missing him by inches, yet leaving the hot, fetid odor of old food. For the past few minutes, however, the dog had been quiet.

He was ready now. His breath was under control. He was as near to the gate as he could get. He surprised himself, carrying as much weight as he did, at how fast he drove up from the ground, released the dog, and charged for the opening. The backs of his legs and buttocks prickled as he waited for the slashing teeth to tear at him … but they never came. He was out of the yard and the gate was closed before he realized he was alone. He didn't turn to look as he dashed for his car, jumped in, and sped for home.

He didn't know exactly why he returned to the Victorian house that morning. Maybe it was to find out why the dog hadn't attacked when he finally let it go. Maybe it was the guilt he felt at a good theory gone bad. In any case, he walked painfully along with his Spaniel at the end of red leash.

It had taken an hour to clean up after he came home a little before 3 a.m. The bite in the arm wasn't as bad as he had first believed, although it had punctured the skin. Behind his legs it was worse, where his pants had lifted exposing skin to the dog's scraping nails. There he found a series of red tracks, some deeper than others, some crossing, forming a number of poorly angled squares. All areas had been washed thoroughly and sprayed with antiseptic. He was grateful that Carol hadn't asked about last night, and hadn't commented on the long sleeve checked shirt and gray dress slacks he wore to breakfast coffee.

He noted the old woman in the yard as he reached the edge of her property. Her veined hand held the screwdriver he had lost earlier that morning.

"Good morning!" he said with a forced casualness. It was an effort to keep his free hand from shaking. He put it in his pocket.

"Morning'," she replied absently, her head scanning the ground.

Extremely awkward for Harold, he pulled his dog, who'd been fretting about the area with her nose to the ground as though she had lost something, closer to the fence so the woman wouldn't miss seeing her. "Say, where's that big dog of yours this morning?"

For the first time she looked in his direction, bringing her hand up to shield her eyes from the east sun. She wore the same blue skirt from the other day with a short sleeve blouse heavily stained from yard work and perspiration.

“Dog? I don’t have a dog. That wasn’t mine they took away this morning.”

Oh God, he thought. He stumbled on words in his rush to get them out. “Not…not your dog? And they took one away, from here? Herold licked his lips furiously. “What, was it hurt or something?”

She came closer to the fence, walking with slow, yard-approved steps. “Dead.” She pointed with the screwdriver, while with her other hand she pressed a thumb into her dentures. “Right over there. Police said it was in a fight. They even had a veterinarian out here working on the dog.” Her face became more animated. “Strangest thing, they said. Went on about no marks on the body except where the dog-tag sliced through the skin and punctured the poor dog’s throat.” She glanced around, a check for eavesdroppers. Satisfied, she added, “It was done by a person, not some animal. Now, who on earth would do something like that?”

Harold’s heart had all but stopped. He could feel himself becoming physically ill. All that time he had spent trying not to kill the dog, to avoid being tripped by the mathematical line. “It’s really a shame." he finally said. It was an afterthought, geared toward himself. His eyes studied the concrete sidewalk.

"Not really a shame." The old woman came closer to the fence as if to share in some well-kept secret. The breeze tugged at her long, silken while hair, sweeping it to the side of her forehead. "Seems this dog's been missing for some time. Now and again, I've seen him taking a short cut through my yard, probably cutting through to the dump behind Oak Street. He's got his own route under and over the fence. I've called the police as soon as I knew, but as yet they haven't been able to catch him."

Somehow those words make him feel better. At least the dog wasn't attached to someone – it had been running free.

"Besides," she continued with a hand-over-mouth giggle, obviously enjoying the control she held over the conversation, "the people who lost him wouldn't want him back anyway." She waited a few seconds for Harold to respond, all the while stretching her tanned wrinkles with a wide grin that suggested an ensuing punchline.

In those few moments, Harold paled. Somehow, he could sense in her expression the seeds to his fall. His question was nothing more than a whisper, "Why?"

She brought her face to within a few inches of Harold's ear. "Had rabies."

*****

ABOUT THE AUTHOR

GLEN BARRERA*, a former partner in a real estate appraisal company, now writes. Over the years he's edited a company newsletter, written short stories and poetry. It wasn't until he divorced a few years ago, however, that he finally found time to take a writing course while working on his first novel,* ***The Assassin Who Couldn't Dance****. His second book,* ***A Capable and Wide Revenge****, is recently published. He is currently working on a third, with the working title,* ***Sweet Peach****.*

www.authorglenbarrera.wordpress.com

MARGARITA MIX

Joseph Mark Brewer

"Please?"

Vincent had never said that word to her until that moment.

"I don't ..."

"Julie, I'm leaving, I just said. Remember?"

He knew no one gave a damn about him, not even Julie, a waitress at the burg's only decent cafe. Small and plump and pretty, red hair and rosy cheeks and so much like an apple he longed to bite. Vincent could not sleep from the thought of her. She poured his coffee and cut extra-large pieces of pie for him. She let him pinch her ass and caress her breasts and kiss her that one time when she and he and Tim the dishwasher found her boss's bottle of Rebel Yell and took turns taking swigs of the foul fire until Tim passed out. Julie's soft whiskey lips became impossible to forget.

"Vincent, it's my only day off ..."

It was that long, slow sigh that had tipped him off to her waning patience. It filled the phone.

"Julie?"

"OK," she said. "Just remember ..."

"I know."

"Vincent."

He felt that beautiful bleat deep down in his soul.

Julie said yes to meeting at the lake after lunch the next day. She finally said yes, despite her bodybuilder boyfriend, all muscles and teeth and golden hair, like a halo.

Vincent hated him.

But – Julie said yes.

That was the important thing.

Vincent was leaving that burg and that college and that life. Not that anyone would know he had been kicked out of college. Not for a couple of days, at least. Not that he cared. It's just that Vincent knew his draft status guaranteed him a ticket to hell.

Canada had always been his plan. And the only person Vincent ever spoke to about this was Father Roger, who said things like "You've got a good head on your shoulders, Vincent. Don't waste it." Father Roger, once movie-star handsome, now had a boozy Rudolph nose under baggy eyelids and recruited his prep school's smart youngsters for a vast, empty Catholic men's college any bishop would have closed decades ago. Father Roger wrangled a freshman scholarship that saved Vincent from the draft board. Vincent knew he could not say no.

But that was September. Now it was April. Canada had always been Vincent's plan.

He had no doubt leaving would be a better deal all around – out of that parochial prison Father Roger insisted he try, out of the dorm and away from the sinister creeps and closet queens and daily Mass and the least Christian brothers he'd ever met. Out of that upstate burg too small to be anything but miserable. No one would ever know if he was in his dorm room or Toronto or Mars. He had no friends there. No one ever called. Or wrote. Not mom. Not Paulie, older by two years but dumber by ten.

Canada was his Oz.

+

Tim the dishwasher said he'd buy Vincent's Volkswagen Beetle. So that became part of the plan. "Talk to Julie, sell the VW," became Vincent's mantra. Julie, the Bug, the Greyhound ticket, have some money left over. Head north.

Money.

"Dough. Greenbacks. Folding money," Vincent heard his dad call it.

Folding money.

Dad.

"Vinnie, someday you'll be a man of the world," his dad said that December while home for winter break. It was the last week his dad was alive, that week before the new decade began. Vincent sat next to his dad's bed and wrote down what his dad said like he was asked to do. Some of his dad's words seemed like so much nonsense. And Vincent sometimes could not hear what was said because of the old man's low emphysemic rumble. Sometimes the bedside radio played the old-time music his mom called "from the war years." Most times the black-and-white TV's sound was down low and dad never watched it but when his mom asked his dad "Francis, want me to turn that off?" his dad always said "Just leave it."

"Vinnie," he said between gasps, "Join the Navy and see the world." He said things like that. And, "It's not the size of the dog in the fight, but the size of the fight in the dog." And, "You never know a man until you've stood in his shoes and walked around in them." Vincent knew that was from that movie about the dad and the girl and her brother and the spooky house. Vincent's dad said he liked the dad in that movie. Not that he resembled him in any way, he had to admit. Even before the cancer, Vincent's dad was no bigger than a jockey, what Uncle Moe called "a banty rooster." Moe was a giant, built like a mountain. Not dad. Moe was "black Irish," all curly hair and five o'clock shadow and fine blue eyes. Dad was all red hair and green eyes and a thin beak of a nose over a square chin. Vincent resembled his dad. It used to bother him.

Vincent's dad liked to say things like "folding money."

Vincent's idea to meet Julie and sell her on his idea, the "Come Join Me" idea—well, offering her a cocktail had sort of been his dad's idea, too. Vincent remembered the cocktail from the time his dad had made sure he wrote down "Go to California."

"It's warm there," he said. "They have a drink there called a margarita. Salty. But damn good. Now don't forget, Vinnie," his dad had said between wheezes no oxygen tank could relieve.

"I won't, Dad," Vincent replied, avoiding his father's gasping gaze. He kept busy writing California Tequila Margarita Lime Califfornya Tekeela Margareeta Lym.

After seeing his dad laid out in a coffin and watching him drop into a grave on New Year's Day, Vincent returned to the burg and the college and the the cold and the snow, wishing he was still sitting next to his dad. He brought the notebook with him. He clutched the notebook. It was the only thing he read. It was the only thing he learned that semester, those things his dad told him to write down.

+

No stretch of the imagination would ever allow Timmons Pond to be called a lake, but that's what some enterprising promoter called it in the burg's boom days before everything went bust. There was nothing left in the burg but the little college and the paper mill, but everyone still called Timmons Pond "the lake."

The burg, too small to even be called a town, sent two men to trim the grass around the lake and tend to the maples and birches nearby. Volunteers cut back the wild azalea, and every March the Boy Scouts marched through, picking up the winter litter. That was three weeks before. That day, the day Vincent planned on saying goodbye to college and the burg, the cold gave way to the promise of April warmth. It was spring and warm and everything Vincent hoped for.

He laid his blanket between the lake's pebbly beach, shiny from the morning rain, and the row of black wrought-iron benches. He turned his face to the sun creeping towards its zenith.

A thermos lay on his lap, warm against his frayed jeans, his fingers still smelling of tequila and lime.

Now he was ready for Julie.

Like a community theater newbie with just the one line, he repeated his plea in as many different ways as he could think of: the oratorical "Come with me, Julie. Let's just go. You and me!" The lover's "Come with me, Julie. Let's just go. You and me!" The beggar's "Come with me, Julie. Let's just go. You and me!"

He wondered if she would take the margarita when he offered it.

Vincent stared at the sky and listened for the low hum of the Ford Pinto Julie was forced to drive. She once said she could not just say no to her parent's charity. She hated the car and Vincent knew she considered his Bug better than her Pinto. Vincent thought about that and the other things she hated about her life that he discovered while dating her. He knew it would be easy to talk her into ditching the Ford and running off with him.

"I'll ask. She'll say yes. We'll seal the deal with a drink. Then we're out of here."

The backfire of a showroom-new Olds 442 turned Vincent's head. Red, black trim, scoop, spoiler, mags.

"The bodybuilder. Damn."

Vincent stared at the muscle car. He watched Julie's head swing to and fro. He realized she was trying to spot any witnesses, as if she was hoping no one was watching. He watched her slip past the barely opened passenger door like a hesitant lawbreaker. Her short quick gate brought her long hair and sweater and jeans and boots and vanilla fragrance and pale white lusciousness to a spot six feet in front of him, her arms folded across her breasts as if naked.

"I'm here. What do you want?"

Vincent watched her eyes fall onto the thermos in his hand. He saw it meant nothing, that it did not even warrant a quizzical look, a "Why did you bring your coffee?" reaction.

"Well?"

Vincent wanted to shout, "Why is he here? Why can't you do just one thing I ask you to without you doing whatever the hell you want?" He wanted to scream, "You were the only thing about this shit town that was any good and I want you to run away with me and you bring that jackass?"

But nothing came out.

Julie's eyes fell to the ground. Vincent knew she'd never willingly look up at him again.

She whispered, "Well?"

The quiet of the question stilled his rage.

Vincent looked down at the thermos and up at Julie's hair falling from her bowed head.

"I just wanted to say fuck you."

Vincent didn't see the shock, the stare, the gaping mouth, the twitching lip, the swift turn and the run back to the boyfriend and the indignant shout and the sudden tears and the rage. Vincent had marched off to his Bug.

He did hear the engine rev and the tires squeal and he smelled rubber on asphalt. But he was in his Bug, safe and secure and just then backing that tin mound of metal into the path of the shiny new 442's gleaming grill. The bodybuilder slammed his foot on the brakes and Julie smacked her forehead onto the dashboard, but Vincent never noticed. He had already pushed the stick shift into first gear and was puttering away, his arm out the window, a one-finger salute proudly pointed toward the sky.

+

Tim the dishwasher was true to his word. Money and title changed hands and after a handshake and a "See ya 'round" Vincent walked to the bus depot.

His plan had been simple. A bus to Canada would keep him out of the draft. Julie would be by his side. He could face anything with her. He had been so sure, once.

In the middle of the depot lobby, among the wooden benches and dingy tile and gum wrappers and cigarette butts, Vincent held his knapsack in one hand, the thermos with his send-off booze in the other, and his eyes scanned the walls for any semblance of a bus schedule. All he wanted to see was Buffalo/Niagara Falls.

But the first word his eyes found and his mind comprehended was San Francisco.

California.

Vincent stepped closer to the sign. Under the San Francisco was all the bus stops: Pittsburgh, Cleveland, Chicago, Kansas City, Denver, Salt Lake City, Reno, Sacramento, San Francisco.

California.

San Francisco.

St. Francis.

Francis.

"Go to California," his dad had told him to write in his notebook. "It's warm there," he had said the week before he died. "They have a drink there, called a margarita. Salty. But damn good. Now don't forget, Vinnie."

Instinct told Vincent to turn his head to the right. He spotted a ticket agent, old and bored and smoking a Pall Mall and staring at nothing.

"Ticket?" Vincent said as he stepped to the counter.

"Where to."

"How much to San Francisco?"

The old man raised a thin yellowed finger and aimed it at a sign behind him, up and to the left.

Vincent's gut clenched.

"You wanna ticket?" The man seemed to say it without moving.

"Yep. San Francisco."

"Leaves in an hour, right over there."

Vincent turned his head again. This time he saw two dirty green metal doors with filthy Plexiglas windows, side by side, under a sign that said "Departures."

"Thanks," Vincent said. He meant it. He took his folding money and paid the agent, picked up his tickets, and stared at them for a long moment before slipping them into his jacket pocket.

Vincent pushed open one of the dirty departure doors and saw two concrete driveways and dividers under an awning. His eyes fell on the trees across the street. Ash. Poplar. Maple. Most were winter naked in the advancing twilight and begging for new buds, standing there behind a row of rusted, slush-coated cars. The day'

April warmth gave way to an early spring chill. But it was dry outside and the wind was still and Vincent's leather jacket was warm enough. Besides, there was margarita in his thermos.

Vincent parked himself on a bench at the foot of the bus station driveway, placed his knapsack at his feet, and opened the thermos. The aromatic tequila salt lime made him salivate. He poured the concoction into the red thermos cup but before he tasted it, Vincent raised the cup to the sky.

"California, here we come. Ain't that right, Francis?"

*****

ABOUT THE AUTHOR

After studying music and a hitch in the navy, ***JOSEPH MARK BREWER*** *settled into traveling and writing. A journalist and author, he writes mysteries and short fiction. Like any good newspaper veteran, he has several unpublished novels. He has recently settled in Austin, Texas, after many years in California. Someday he hopes to resume a life on the road.*

WEATHER THE STORM

Neil Newton

Dr. Messenberg slapped some papers on his desk in front of me. "I suppose you knew you'd get this," he grumbled.

I just smiled. Being the star of the linguistics department I usually got what I wanted. I had to admit this grant was a bit more spectacular than anything I'd previously proposed. It was, by all standards, the linguistic study to trump all past linguistic studies.

I was at the end of a long line of dialect geographers, all searching for the secret of how a dialect is contained in a geographical area. Like any fringe discipline dialect geography has become an orgy of different core subjects coming together to create … something. Geographers, socio-linguists, linguists, statisticians, economists. The works. I'd been handed a major mystery. Though most laymen were convinced that American English was leading toward total standardization, thanks to the English used by television talking heads, the reality was that there was a previously unexplainable mystery that had all linguists talking. It was a vowel shift, a strange pronunciation of a vowel that had no known origin. It hadn't come from any source anyone could identify.

While I know that dialect geography isn't exciting and hearing about this epic mystery would make most people's eyes glaze over, the truth is that for those that study mankind, it is a fascinating change in the history of how our languages work.

I look at my work this way: In a world of chaos, lack of cohesion, entropy and other forces, what makes people speak with the same dialect in a geographical area? What's an even better question is, what forms the borders between those areas? Is it a gradual change or are there sharp geographical divisions in dialect?

What makes a phrase spoken by one person become part of slang that is on everyone's lips within a year? Why is all soda called *pop* in some places and *coke* in other places? Why would certain socio-economic classes of people rather die than leave off the final "g" in words ending with "ing"? These mysteries reflect our history and our culture and tell the story of a nation.

And why would a small part of the population suddenly pronounce a vowel differently for no apparent reason? What historical forces made this happen? I was going to find out.

It's been a question that has plagued all dialect geographers. And I'd developed a mathematical model to explain the way accents morph into a new dialect across a physical geographical plain. Unlike many of my predecessors, I'd injected a strong dose of economics into my model, treating areas like Chicago differently than a small city like Mobile. A large metropolitan area that has people commuting to work from miles away does its magic on a much wider area of people in terms of their dialect.

I'd decided that I'd put my model to a real test. Up till then I had done some dry runs, targeting small areas of perhaps thirty miles. This time I would show my stuff. I knew that I'd be hated, both for my success and my arrogance. I was used to that. Solving the mystery of the odd vowel pronunciation in only a few states would be my ticket to scholarly fame.

My life didn't start with the success I'd experienced in academe. My childhood was what I'd have to call average until I was seven, when I started having headaches which recurred several times a week. They only became worse as time went by. When I began having mild hallucinations my mother, a nurse, decided that things were serious. She was proved right; they found a benign tumor that was still small enough to be removed without significant damage.

The surgery was a success, but I was never to be the same. The headaches continued though I was able to fight them off with migraine medicine. The hallucinations, which had been horrific before the operation, became an occasional problem. But they never completely disappeared. When they would plague me, I'd spend a day or two seeing people that weren't there. Usually they were people I'd never seen before, but occasionally I'd see a face repeated. That made me think the people were real. Despite my panic, it was easy for my parents to pass it off as the after effects of my surgery and they'd ignore my childish expressions of fear in the way adults do. "They're only dreams," my mother would say. My father would tell me to stop being silly. "It's your vivid imagination." They ignored my complaints of flashing lights, long tunnels, and the peculiar halos that sometimes surrounded the heads of these strangers in my mind. As a child I had no reference to describe the odor of what I later came to identify as sulphur.

+

I walked out of the humanities building into a beautiful spring day. I'd been obsessing about the logistics of the study. In my mind was a map of the study area, with the city as a node in the middle and growing areas of suburban settlement moving out from the center. I played out the gradual changes in accent and language elements, seeing the changes in language that I knew would be there.

Like an expectant father I hurried to the computer center to run the model, even though I knew what the results would be. I walked back to the terminal room and brought up the program; for the sake of shaking out any problems it was being run over a small sample of test data taken from a small city sixty miles from the university. The program had been developed to show language change over a geographical area. This rendered the results as shifting colored lines. I could see the geographical area we were targeting as a series of lines moving across from the inner city to the outlying areas. The lines changed colors as the dialect of one area morphed slowly to the next incrementally changed dialect of a new geographical node. The change was gradual, moving through all the gradations, through the primary colors and the non-primary colors. There was an expected series of color change if the model was working correctly, something I knew would happen, this being the tenth time I'd run it this week.

I smiled as I saw everything moving according to plan. I was keeping the model in my head, following it as I'd done many times. Then I heard someone call to me. I turned to see one of my students. We waved and I turned back to the screen.

To my horror something had gone terribly wrong. The one color I didn't want to see was pink. That meant the model had failed. And all of the lines, the entire study, was a bright pink that screamed failure. I had run this model on computers a hundred times. I had played it out in my head repeatedly. I leaned back and felt a wave of dizziness come over me and I knew in a second that a headache was coming on. While I rarely got headaches, the sad fact was that what constituted a headache for me made the worst migraine seem tame.

I ran to my car, falling into the driver's seat and immediately reaching for my pills in the glove compartment. I pulled out a bottle of water and downed the pills quickly, hoping I could stave off the worst of the headache.

I sat there, colors washing across my sight. A ghost image of my model floated at the edge of my vision, still an accusatory pink. It was time to go; I started the car and raced out of the parking lot.

+

I didn't go in to the office the next day. I needed to start interviewing my linguistic research interns if the study was to start on time but, with a headache of this magnitude, that was impossible. As I lay in bed, I began to see colors in my right eye.

It was a migraine plus whatever leftovers remained from my surgery. The pain was tolerable, thanks to some excellent medication. I tried my best not to think of my timetable for the project and all the people I wasn't interviewing that day.

I could handle pain; I was so used to it. What was really eating at me was my odd experience with my model. It was foolproof; we'd tested it in computer simulations and it gave the same results no matter who ran it. So why did it fail? Or did it fail? Was the perception of a complete shutdown of the model due to my surgery years ago? I'd had hundreds of episodes where I stood with people and saw something that no one else saw, usually followed by a headache. Maybe it was just a biological anomaly in my brain. I'd spent my whole life in fear that somehow my surgery would ruin me. No more star of the linguistics department. No more grants. No more lording it over my jealous and belligerent brother at Christmas.

My brother had been a sore subject all my life. He'd laughed when he heard I was going into linguistics, saying, "You'll be eating beans for the rest of your life. That's if you get a job teaching in the first place." It had been sweet going back home in the last few years, wearing a Rolex watch and driving a Mercedes. Being a prodigy, writing books, working for computer companies on their voice recognition software, and guest speaking had changed my life completely. My brother had a used tire store. He had thought it would make him a bundle and that he'd be able to open a hundred stores, becoming the tire king of Philadelphia. Somehow it had never worked out. I knew it ate at him.

When I'd come home from the hospital as a child I'd spent quite a while with bandages on my head, going to physical therapy and being generally creepy. My brother called me Frankenstein for years, even when the surgery was a distant memory. Being a big success gave me a chance to look him in the eye and laugh. I was getting mine back.

+

The next day I was almost functional. Even if I hadn't been pain free, I'd have gone in. There was a brief time window for this study; it had to be up and running within a short time. That meant that I had to start interviewing students for the positions I'd have to fill. Each of my interns would have to work with other interns to track the various changes in language as the team moved across the geographical area of the study.

I went into the office early and ran my model again. No problems; it was perfect. I ran it again three times before I convinced myself that the failure was due to an anomaly. I lay back in my chair and closed my eyes, drifting off into a state of semi-sleep. Suddenly there was a knock on my door that shattered the uneasy reverie I had fallen into. I opened my eyes and took a deep breath. I knew I had to be on my game for these interviews; even one unperceptive turd could ruin the study with incorrect data and inept conclusions. There would be very little time to remedy any mistakes made.

My first interviewee was a young woman who I'd had in my semantics class. Her movements were quick and jerky; a twitchy type. She looked at me with a face full of earnestness as I sat down behind my desk. I immediately disliked her; I wasn't a fan of idealism but I needed interviewers so I put my bias aside. I saw that she held the abstract of the study; it was dog-eared and rumpled, giving me the impression that she'd attempted to memorize it. I winced.

I looked down at her references. "Susan Boyd. I see that you've read the abstract. What do you think makes you the type of person to be an interviewer in this study? I'll start by saying that we have a really small window of time. We aren't in position to perform re-dos on gathering this information. It could kill the entire study. Now what do you see as your role?"

She straightened her back. "I thought about this last night. I would suggest the use of minimal pairs combined with readings of—"

"Hold it. Did you read the abstract?"

"Several times."

"Did you read the part about the importance of commuting to work daily to the city from semi-rural areas? Did you read the part about retirees moving to the rural areas from out of state? The socio-economic characteristics of the speaker?"

Her nose twitched. I found that very disturbing. "Yes. I did read that. But the classical field work emphasizes the interviewing process…"

"I'm aware of the importance of the interviewing process. Of course we have to interview people to measure change in dialect over a geographical area. But I know that in the abstract I emphasized a more agile approach, including elements of socio-linguistics and economics. Not just vanilla pronunciation issues and vowel shifts. This is a bit more subtle than the classic interviewing techniques you learned about in Linguistics 101."

I suddenly had the awful feeling that she was going to cry. Her mouth twitched. "I would really appreciate the opportunity to work with you. You're considered the most cutting edge scholar in the field. I realize that I have a lot to learn but I will read the abstract again and make sure that I look for the elements that you're seeking."

I'm not big on politeness, which has been my downfall in the past. In the end the supply of potential interns wasn't large. While I wanted to tell this oh-so-sincere soi-disant scholar that she wasn't intelligent or experienced enough to tell the difference in dialect between a Chinese monk and a southern Baptist, I had to be realistic. *She can be taught*, I told myself, not quite believing it.

+

I interviewed five more. One was perfect; the rest not so wonderful. Susan Boyd was right. My work was cutting edge. But as good as that was, it also guaranteed that the average linguistics student was more than likely to misunderstand what I was trying to establish with this study.

What caused my department chairman to fall in love with me was the basis of the study. Though for most people linguistics is like watching paint dry, for linguists I was chasing after the Holy Grail. Consider this: most people believe that American English is becoming standardized across geographical boundaries. Put in simpler terms, the idea is that watching the news, movies and television would drum the standard American dialect into everyone's head until, eventually, all Americans would sound approximately the same.

But nature abhors a vacuum. Sometime in the mid-twentieth century there was significant change in the pronunciation of certain vowels in five Midwest states. This was not caused by the talking heads on the news; the variation in the way this vowel is pronounced is different than the dialect laymen call "American Standard", the dialect used by new anchors.

So why was this happening? No one knows. And what I had in mind was to find the geographical boundaries of this linguistic oddity. And once I did, I could use statistical analysis to find the most likely source of the vowel shift, to define what caused it. The implications were enormous: if my model worked well it could be used to analyze other dialect anomalies across the country, or even across the world.

+

In the end I did choose Susan Boyd. Enthusiasm was better than an indifferent student simply wanting extra credit and a few bucks. There were two more, one a Masters student named Daniel who seemed to get the idea of the study, the other a linguistics student close to getting his M.S. His name, Spike, worried me until I found that he was more than able to follow the basis of my study, I took them to dinner a few days before we left for our jumping off point in western Wisconsin. That would be the place that we'd staked out as the western edge of the vowel shift.

I watched them closely as we worked at our Thai food. Any kind of conflict could make a study into a nightmare. Data collection takes focus and petty spats can make that into oatmeal. Though the outcome was still murky, I was happy to see that this crew was getting along. Susan Boyd seemed like she was in heaven, trading witty repartee with two male students way above her level. By her second glass of wine she was laughing and, to my great disgust, flirting with Daniel, the graduate student.

I was drinking scotch, the drink of writers and intellectuals. As I watched the three of them I got a strange sensation in my head. It wasn't like a migraine coming on but more like some of the sensations I'd had after my surgery when I was a kid. I saw the far wall recede and then rush forward as though it was going to hit me in the face. The three students became indistinct, going in and out of focus.

What came next scared me. I saw people who were not in the restaurant, popping in and out of existence every other second. I took a good gulp from my scotch, hoping it would clear my head, but my phantom guests continued their disappearing and reappearing act. I stared at them, though they didn't seem to notice me at all. Not a strange thing for non-existent men and woman to do, I told myself.

"Are you okay?" Daniel asked.

"Uh…yes. Fine"

"You look strange."

"I always look strange." I did my best to smile while I watched my phantom friends act like Christmas lights.

"I'm just wondering if you need to go home. There's no color in your face."

I had been staring at the phantoms the whole time. I was scared but not half as scared as I was about to be. One of them got an odd look on his face. He popped out and when he returned, he was pointing at me. In seconds all of them were staring back at me. Another pointed in my direction.

I stood up quickly, knocking over my scotch. The three students stared at me. I was breathing hard, looking away from my phantoms in the hope that shaking my head would make them go away.

I looked up slowly. I got a brief glimpse of them. In that second I saw the one that had pointed at me move his hand laterally. And that was the last thing I saw for the next few hours.

+

I woke up in the hospital. My first image was of a nurse standing over me. I sat up with a jerk, the fear I'd felt just before I'd passed out still at work in my mind.

"Whoa!" the nurse said. "You need to lie back. We don't know what's wrong with you."

For a second I debated whether I should tell her that I'd seen phantom people while I was eating green curry, just to see the look on her face; in the end I decided that they needed to know what had happened if they were going to help me. I followed her order and lay back down. "I guess I should tell you I had a brain tumor as a child. I've had odd … episodes all my life. Nothing much lately. Tonight I saw—not saw, but it seemed like I saw people in the restaurant. They faded in and out from my sight. They weren't there. I know that."

She stood stock still for a second. "I'm going to get the doctor."

Ten minutes later a doctor walked into the room. He pulled up one of the visitor's chairs and sat near to my bed. "Nurse Cortez told me what you told her. I appreciate the honesty because we could have taken hours to find out your basic problem. This surgery you had as a child; what were the aftereffects?"

"Headaches. Sight issues. Hallucinations. Balance problems. I still get mega migraines but not that often."

"What about the hallucinations?"

"Recently? Rarely. Tonight was an unwelcome reminder of my childhood."

"Did you feel pain when you had this hallucination?"

"No. Not pain. But it was like there was some pressure in my head and I felt disoriented."

"I think that we'll need to do an MRI. I'm sure there are some physical abnormalities in your brain from the surgery."

"But why now after all these years?"

He spread his hands. "The brain is still mostly unknown territory. Changes take place in everyone's brain as they grow. In your case there's probably some damage that is being exacerbated by any number of factors as you get older."

"Oh God. I thought I was done with this."

"I wouldn't panic if I were you. Remember that you had hallucinations. You didn't have a haemorrhage or sight loss. Have you been under a lot of stress lately?"

"Frankly … yes."

"It could be that. Let us do the MRI and we'll see."

"Is there a chance the tumor could have regrown?"

"Possible but unlikely. You went through this the first time so you'll remember. The symptoms of having a large tumor are a little more spectacular than one anomaly involving hallucinations."

"Okay."

He put his hand on my arm. "I wouldn't worry. Let's see what we find."

+

For those that have never experienced an MRI, it's like sitting near a bad conga circle that can't keep time. The sounds that you have to endure are awful, much like someone is outside the machine with a hammer. What's worse is that you can't move enough to make yourself more comfortable. Forty-five minutes of this hell before I was able to get up and stretch my legs.

I went back to setting up the study, meeting daily with the three students to go over the plan. For Susan, in her inexperience, I had to emphasize the use of intuition and statistical methods to validate that our results were significant. I was happy to see that she seemed to be becoming more relaxed and even brought some good ideas to the table. Considering my health issues I was going to have to rely heavily on the judgment of my interviewers.

A week later I met with my doctor. I found that I was more nervous that I thought I would be. It had been years since my tumor had been an issue and I supposed that I was living in denial, thinking that I was over the hard part when I had no reason to believe that. Over the previous week I had remembered things that my doctors had said when I was child about possible "complications." Somewhere along the line I had buried my fears and ignored the possibilities. Undoubtedly this was due to my parents' influence and their own fears of admitting their child was less than healthy.

I sat down across the desk from my doctor. He studied me, his face darkening. "Are you okay?"

"This is very undignified. As you may have realized I'm not very tolerant of frustration. People often find me irritating. This *problem* threatens my work and my reputation."

I became more annoyed because he laughed. "Excuse me," he said. "Most of my patients are consumed by fear. That's a perfectly reasonable reaction. You just seem pissed off."

"Let's just say I've had it with the whole brain tumor thing. I was a freak when I was a kid. My own brother picked on me mercilessly. I've made a name for myself and want the brain tumor and any residual effects to just go away."

"I understand. Really. I was a nerd as a child. I know what demons little kids can be. But I think you should feel relieved. I've looked over the MRI results and I can't see that there has been any degradation in your brain's structure near the site of the surgery; your brain has healed well. I got to look at your imaging from when you were a child. I can't see any problems. If there was a consistent, growing change in your brain you'd have far more serious episodes than one hallucination. If there was a real problem it would have manifested itself by now."

"So what was the *manifestation* I experienced the other night?"

"Stress. Indigestion. Sinus issues. You do have a volatile region in your brain. It will show itself when other factors enter the picture."

"So what is your prognosis?"

"I would guess that you may have episodes like this again in your life but not often. You should go ahead and continue making your name in your field."

I snorted. "I guess I have to accept that."

"Are you unhappy? Would you rather that I told you that your tumor has returned?"

"Onward, ever onward!" I answered. "Ours not to reason why, ours but to do and die." I smirked. "Is that positive enough for you?"

"Glass half empty, eh?"

"Being a freak and missing school for two years has a negative effect on the psyche".

"Understandable. A lot of my patients don't have a good outlook on life."

We stared at each other for a moment. "Well, I would like to have you come back in a month to check on you. You never know about these things."

"I suppose." I had to love this doctor. He encouraged me on one hand and covered his ass on the other.

+

I left feeling angry. I didn't have any reason to be. It seemed I was okay. Yet I started having feelings I hadn't had since I was a child; feelings I had suppressed for years and was now being reminded of.

My medical issues had put me back a few days; I flew out to Madison to meet my team. The previous couple of days they had been interviewing people according to my schedule. There were recordings I had to go over. I got there at night and was so bummed out that I just went to sleep, not being my usual bulldog self. Susan Boyd wanted to show me what she had accomplished and was crestfallen when I begged off from drinks in the hotel bar and went to bed.

The next morning my mood wasn't much better. I had had nightmares the night before, something that had plagued me as a child. I was hoping that as long as I hung on, things would go back to normal. I hadn't realized how much I'd enjoyed being a star at something. It had eclipsed the sickly freak I'd been as a child.

I did my best to put my mind on autopilot. I'd hidden my anger and disgust with humanity all my adult life by playing a part. I could do it again. My team came to my room and I ordered room service that included two bottles of wine. I wanted to maintain the image that we were elite; that this was a party for our success, even though we hadn't succeeded yet.

I lay on my bed and listened to the interviews. In this phase of the study we were concentrating on what I felt to be the most fascinating part of the vowel shift. Think of the word cat. We learn in school that the vowel sound in that word is a short "a." It's the same sound in words like "that" or "bat". What had happened in several areas from western New York State to western Wisconsin was that many people had started, during the sixties, to pronounce the work "cat" like "Key-et": two syllables where only one actually exists, with a long "e" sound inserted in the first syllable.

Not quite a phenomenon with the reach of the Russian revolution, but a mystery nonetheless. Why did this happen? No one was sure. But I would be certain once I gathered all the data. I would trace the change back in time using data collected over decades. And I'd find the "patient zero" that had brought this change to the English Language.

Each recording was preceded by a short verbal introduction by the interviewer, usually highlighted by some condescending remarks about the interviewee. "If he had four teeth I'd be surprised." "She made dinner table decorations out of light bulbs. She wrote down directions on how to make them, like we cared."

I smiled. Condescension always brought up my spirits. I followed the geographical trail in my mind as I heard each recording. I knew when and where these recordings were taken; it was part of a line west out of the Madison metropolitan area. The first ten or so recordings had the characteristic vowel shift. The word "That" became "The-yet", the "y" sounding like a long "e".

Around the sixth recording I started to get odd sensations in my head. What alarmed me most is that these were the same sensations I'd experienced in the restaurant a little over a week before. I'd been visualizing the pattern of dialect change in my head. As expected the odd vowel shift had begun to weaken slightly as the interviews moved west. Then there was a sharp pain and I heard an accent that, to my trained ear, sounded like an east Tennessee dialect.

I sat up suddenly. "Where did that come from?" I asked my team.

Daniel stared at me. "Where did what come from?"

"That fucking accent. Is this a joke?"

"What are you talking about?"

I got a bad feeling. I was good at reading people and Daniel seemed panicked and angry. With my hand shaking, I pointed at the recorder. "Replay that last interview from the beginning."

Daniel rushed to comply, stealing glances in my direction. He went back to the beginning of the interview and hit play. I heard the interviewer, Susan in this case, asked the subject to say the word "rat." What I heard was an East Tennessee accent as I had before. No Midwestern vowel shift. Not even close to the right dialect I was expecting. We were in Wisconsin and the interviewee was speaking with the wrong accent entirely.

"You don't hear that?" I screamed. All three of them jumped up.

Susan put her hands out. “What is wrong, Jeff? It’s the vowel shift, just like we expected.

I felt my world moving out from under me. “It’s an East Tennessee accent!” I screamed again.

Susan’s eyes widened. “What are you saying? We’re not in Tennessee! All the interviews were done here in Wisconsin. Where do you think we are?”

I tried to speak, but what could I possibly say? Either I was being played by all three of them, an unlikely scenario, or I was going insane. Or perhaps my brain was shutting down, finally being consumed by the hole they’d created when they removed my tumor. I could almost see it happening in my head; the angry maw of the surgery site eating the rest of my brain.

I sat down and poured a large scotch and knocked it back in one gulp. That didn’t seem to do any good so I drank another four fingers or so. And then I looked up. I saw the same people I’d seen in the restaurant, the phantoms. Only this time they weren’t popping in and out of existence. They were solid and they were staring at me with horrified looks on their faces. The man who had pointed at me back in the restaurant said something to a woman in the group, in a language I didn’t recognize. Training took over; I began analyzing the language for its characteristics and probable language group. It sounded somewhat guttural. But in the end I realize that it wasn't similar enough to any language I'd ever heard for me to even coming close to identifying it.

They all walked toward me. "You see us, don't you?" one of them said.

I smiled. If I was going to go insane I would do it in style. "Scotch?" I lifted my glass, offering to share my libation with them. "This is excellent. Straight from Islay. I recommend it."

The man who'd pointed at me at the restaurant smiled. "I'm Seth. I think we need to talk."

"What about my team here. They are…" I'd turned around as I was speaking. My "team" had lain down on the floor and gone to sleep.

"They won't remember anything. There will be logical narrative in their minds that explains the time they spent on the project. You don't need to worry about them."

"If I'm crazy then what does it matter what you say?"

"I can see why you might think that. The best thing to do now is to take you to our offices and explain things to you. I think there will be some relief from hearing the truth."

"The truth?" I asked. "The truth of my life?"

"Actually, yes."

I started to pour another drink when Seth waved his hand to stop me. “Just relax.” He smiled. “We have better stuff where we’re going”.

Before I could say anything I felt a sense of disorientation, as though I was spinning. The next moment found me on what could only be described as a couch. I sat up and Seth stepped into the room. He pulled up a chair and sat next to me. “We put you to sleep before we brought you here. Our method of transportation takes some getting used to. I felt you had gone through enough at that point.”

“How long have I been sleeping?”

“About six hours. You were exhausted.”

“You realize I’m having a debate in my head as to the reality of this. Maybe this is just another hallucination.”

“I think that you’ll find all of this to be real once you recover your … equilibrium.”

“*If* I do reacquire my equilibrium.”

“We want to help you do that.”

“We?”

“Guess it’s time to spill my guts.”

“It could be useful.”

“Imagine this. Throughout the universe there is a … well I’d have to compare it to the weather. Imagine that stable reality and probability are the base state of all the universe. But like a sunny day with a beautiful blue sky there will come a weather front; cloudy days, rain, hail. So like the coming of a period of bad weather we have a period of what can only be called inconsistent probability. Or changing probability."

"What?"

He reached into his pocket, pulled out a piece of paper and began shredding it. After a couple of minutes he had a wadded ball of paper, totally shredded. He smiled at me. Then he threw the paper up in the air, letting the pieces fly in different directions.

"Weeeee!" I offered.

"Yes. It is a bit child-like. But I'll ask you if you see a pattern to the distribution of the pieces."

"No. That type of thing is, while not quite random, it's not subject to a strong pattern. Like dice, it's virtually random."

"Exactly. Imagine if the whole world was like shreds of paper thrown up in the air. Would there be dialects spoken by millions of people in one area? Or would randomness create what you would call an idiolect for each person? Am I using the right word?"

"If you mean that every man, woman and child would have their own way of speaking then you're using the right word."

"Yes. In fact it's possible that everyone would have their own language. And even that wouldn't be stable. And that's what the earth is going through now. Dialects, movement, houses, mountains, even people. With varying probability things change, sometimes drastically. This hit the earth around twenty years ago. We can control some of the larger things. We can stop houses from moving or cars from turning into mud; this involves the physical safety of everyone on earth. But there are smaller things that are harder to control. Things of the mind, like language. Or memory. For those things we have to convince your minds that certain things are happening. Ironically one of these things is language. There is the story of Babel in your Bible. Without our help no one would be able to understand each other. In reality, everyone has their own dialect, as long as this probability storm persists."

"So you're saying that comprehensible language is an illusion? And we're being convinced that it is real?"

"Yes. I know that is upsetting to you."

"What about my friends. My colleagues. Is the linguistics department an illusion? Does it exist?"

"You are guided to believe that it exists. The same with your colleagues. And so it does. We strive to create artifacts like a linguistics department because such things existed before this probability storm. The reality is that if we didn't look after you, the meaning, purpose, even the members of department might change. Or the department would cease to exist. You'd all wander off to do different things that suddenly became reality for that moment. Or some of you might disappear. This is so complex there's no way I can accurately describe the scope of the problem."

"And you and your friends. Who are you?"

"There is a race of what you define as Aliens. This problem of shifting reality occurs all over the Galaxy, like dark cloud that moves from one place to another. Or should I say, clouds. There is more than one of them. Many races have been destroyed by these clouds. Either they are physically harmed by changes in the topography … rocks grow out of the ground or move killing the inhabitants of a planet. Or changes in the mind cause insanity as reality changes. The race I'm talking about has made it their mission to allow races to mature enough to join the league of races. They saw the potential disaster on earth years before it came. They sent their own here and began to train humans to protect humanity."

"I'm confused. How does this race of Aliens avoid the effects of the changes? Do they create illusions for their own race to keep them from going insane?"

He smiled. "It's a matter of maturity of the race. Once you reach a certain stage in your evolution these reality shifts don't affect you. You create your own reality within the pockets of unreality. It's like having an umbrella in the rain."

"Are you human?"

He laughed. "Of course. I was raised and trained by … we call them Ascendants. Their name in their own language would be difficult for you to pronounce."

"So what happens to me?"

"We can work on your brain. You'd forget everything you've seen. Though there is the risk that it won't work. Your surgery when you were a child is the reason you're able to see things that other humans can't."

"Great."

"There's another option. One I hope you'll consider seriously. The work we do for the human race is important. You have a unique perspective. You could help us."

"What could I do?"

"A lot. There are other people like you. Sometimes it isn't even due to an accident or illness. Some people have brains that are constructed oddly and they see pieces of reality. We need those people to help us do our work. You can introduce them to the new reality." He smiled.

I hung my head. He looked at me with what was clearly pity. "You have to give me some time." I croaked. "I can't give you an answer now."

"I didn't expect you would. Why don't you rest? We have a room set up for you. Take a couple of days. If you have any questions, please ask for me."

"Okay."

I was led to a room where I simply lay down. There was a bottle of scotch on a table near the bed but I didn't feel that even alcohol would help me in the state I was in. I lay down on the bed and fell asleep.

+

I woke up and, looking at the clock, I realized I'd slept for seventeen hours. I went out into the hall; a man I hadn't seen before walked by. "Are you hungry?"

"Actually, yes."

"Let me take you to the cafeteria."

I grunted and let him lead me. There were only a few people in the cafeteria; it seemed I had slept passed lunch. I sat down and they brought me some pasta. I was hungrier than I thought, putting away my meal in ten minutes. Another bowl appeared before me and I got through it in five minutes.

I was licking my bowl when Seth showed up. "Good to see you have an appetite. Have you given any thought to what I discussed with you yesterday?

"Well, it occurs to me that if I decide to go for the mind meld, I'll be an expert in dialects that don't exist. A noble pursuit. One worthy of all my education. Which by the way is an illusion as well. I'm not sure I could go back to being an automaton. Could you give me more of an idea what I would have to do for the Ascendants?"

+

Six months passed quickly. I found that in addition to being taught the truth of how the universe worked, there were modifications done on my mind and body. I wasn't able to create a personal reality but I could affect people's thoughts if I needed to protect people from reality. Most of the illusion, including the one that created the perception of language groups, was handled by devices provided by the Ascendants. I would only intervene if it was needed when someone like me started seeing past the illusions. I couldn't really call the devices the ascendants used "machines" because they were part living tissue. The complexity of what I was learning was daunting and I sometimes wondered if I wanted to go through with it. I had learned that my training would last for at least a decade. Just about everything I had to learn was so far beyond my understanding that I might as well have been back in kindergarten.

My so-called career in the linguistics department was resolved easily; as far as any of my colleagues and students were concerned, they'd never met me. At first I was horrified at the thought of manipulating people's memories but, after six months of training, I learned that fooling my old colleagues was child's play compared to what was done in an hour by people like Seth. And it was all necessary.

On a whim I took a walk through a shopping mall to listen to the dialects being used. I was horrified for the first few minutes. I was able to access their thoughts and could follow their conversations but the reality was a mess; it was like a thousand languages were being spoken in that one area, there was no consistency between the languages, no Germanic or romance group. There was only a mess of random noise that meant something to the speaker. I found my former linguistic expertise, or my pretention of expertise, embarrassing.

I tried to console myself with the knowledge that I was really going to accomplish something with my new work and that I was no longer a puppet. Yet somehow I still found myself harbouring a small resentment that I'd been allowed by the universe to fool myself into thinking I was a rising star in my world and that it was all a lie.

I felt a now familiar sensation. No, not the result of my brain surgery. It was a "come hither" from Seth. He wanted to discuss my progress and where I might be most useful. I wasn't able to transport myself, yet. I had to live with the indignity of having to ask someone to do it for me. I smiled at the vestiges of my overblown pride and wondered if it would ever go away.

*****

ABOUT THE AUTHOR

***NEIL DOUGLAS NEWTON** was born and raised in New York City, growing up in Bayside, a small community in Queens. He began writing as a child, creating vivid characters to entertain friends and family. Neil is also a musician who can often be seen indulging his interest in the arcane art of finger picking guitar. He has written several songs which he has performed at local venues.*

Neil currently lives in Knoxville, Tennessee, with his wife, writer Elizabeth Horton-Newton, and an assortment of rescued dogs and cats. Parent to four and grandparent to five, he and his wife enjoy traveling worldwide.

*Neil is presently working on his next novel, **Unraveling the Coil**, based on the science and philosophy of Nikola Tesla.*

THE NIGHT PASSENGERS

Charlie Flowers & Hannah Haq

'Fucking hell. You going to a pyjama party or what?'

The man in the zipped-up Adidas tracksuit top plonked himself down into the train seat and glared at the Muslim girl sitting opposite him. He opened the ringpull on his can of beer with a soft plishing sound, took a sip, and shook his head.

Neither of the two would know for many weeks that they'd both thought exactly the same thought as they clapped eyes on each other, and it was this. 'Oh HERE we go.'

So each looked at the other, as they sat on facing seats across a table on the 8 p.m. Intercity from Liverpool Street station, and a host of prejudices and pen-portraits fled across their minds.

He looking at her: one of them hijabis. Fussy camel-hump headscarf. Desert Paki clothes. Reading the Independent for God's sake.

Her looking at him: football hooligan. Adidas top zipped up to the jawline. Can of beer. Yob.

She tutted and rustled her copy of the Independent, using it to ward him off.

It didn't work. He spoke. 'Since we're going to be stuck on this train for a while, what's your name and where you from?'

She lowered the paper. 'My name is Ruby. From Colchester. Do I know you?'

'Gary. Maybe you do.'

'Do I now. Where from?'

'Around.'

Ruby gazed more closely at him. And suddenly he burst into song. 'Ruby Ruby Rubeee!' he laughed.

She narrowed her eyes. 'Haven't heard *that* one before. Anyway, it says in here that Garys will be extinct by 2050 so I wouldn't laugh too hard.'

Gary shot the look back. 'Funny. Anyway, my friends call me Gal.'

'Gawel?'

'GAL. G-A-W. I mean L. Gal short for Gary.'

'Ah.'

'Colchester.' Gary said. 'So you're an Essex bird then.'

Ruby laughed. 'I suppose I am.'

The train whooshed through Romford in a blur of lights, and then Ruby narrowed her eyes at Gary. 'OK then Mr Gary, where are you off to?'

Gary took a long drag on his can of beer. 'Chelmsford, luv. Going to a meet.'

'A meet?'

'Yeah. Casuals United. I joined them when the English Defence League went rubbish.'

Ruby's eyes narrowed further. 'Oh is that right? Meeting more racists to plan burning mosques and throwing pigs' heads around? Bet you're proud, sir. Bet you're proud.'

The man on the table across the aisle rustled his paper and buried his face in it.

Gary put his can down on the table between them. 'Ruby. We have never burned a mosque. Or done anything stupid with bloody pigs heads. We march, and we protest, and that's all.'

Ruby leant forward. 'Right then Gary. Tell me in three short sentences why you joined and what you think you're gonna achieve.'

Gary thought about it for a bit, took a sip from his can. And then thought some more.

Ah, gotchya, Ruby thought to herself. You haven't thought this through.

And then he spoke.

'One. Anjem Choudary and his goons. Two. Sharia courts. Three. Home-grown terrorism.'

And now he was on a roll. 'Also, Ruby, when I joined London EDL, they were different. Multiracial, Muslim friendly. Half of them had Muslim girlfriends.'

'You're kidding.'

'No Ruby, I'm not. Anyway that all changed and the EDL got silly and full of idiots. It's all about Casuals United now.'

There was a lull in the conversation as they both thought their separate thoughts.

The train thundered on.

By now the relentless push and pull of the train matched the ebb and flow of drunken city boys staggering down the aisle towards the on board bar. The sight of Savile Row suits and the stench of stale smoke permeated the carriage. As if by magic, a stocky twenty something barrow boy brushed past Ruby, can of Stella in hand. He stopped. 'Alriiight darling?'

If Patrick Bateman and Michael Barrymore had a bastard child, this chap would surely have been it, Ruby thought to herself.

Ruby raised her eyebrows, glanced at his faux diamond dollar sign cufflinks and let out a sigh. And at this point, all three sets of eyes locked. Ruby noticed that Gary's eyes had fixed on the drunken city boy, and ever so slightly, his head had tipped left and right in a "no". And Gary's eyes had gone as cold as stone chips.

Without further ado the City boy left sharpish, stumbling away.

Ruby wondered how Gary had done that.

And Gary flashed Ruby a sheepish smile. 'Does that happen often, y'know with you being all veiled up and that?'

'Veil? It's a Hijab!' snapped Ruby, rousing the attention of the carriage. She cast her eyes around. The man across the aisle spilt his cup of premium grade Colombian coffee in a frantic attempt to avoid her gaze.

'OK. The Heeeeeejab,' Gary repeated half mockingly. He placed the near empty can of beer on the table and stretched out his legs. 'Let me guess. Some fella made you wear it.'

Ruby shook her head. Not again, she thought. This wasn't the first time some white knight had attempted to save her from the savages of the Modern Muslimah dress code. 'It's time for Hijab 101 for the unenlightened I see,' she muttered to herself.

'What was that?' said Gary. Ruby realised she'd muttered it to herself alright, but slightly too loud. She cleared her throat and the man over in the next aisle brought his paper up again as a shield.

And Ruby leant across the plastic table and spoke.

'Number one, Gary, I wear it because ***I*** want to.'

'Number two, my family are dead against it. Surprising, but they are,'

'And three, it's bloody convenient for bad hair days.'

Gary said nothing. He turned to look out the window; his eyes fixated on the blur of flashing lights trackside. He looked back at Ruby. And then silence.

'Well that shut him up,' Ruby thought to herself.

And at that point he train whined to a sudden halt, the sheer force jolting the passengers into their newspapers and laptops. There was a rustle of passive-aggressive cursing.

'Drrrring'. The train PA system chimed in for yet another delay.

'*Apologies. We have been held here at a red signal...*' announced senior conductor Kevin.

Ruby smiled at hearing his voice.

Kevin was Ruby's favourite, often asking babies for valid tickets or men in pinstripe suits if they 'was the one that did it'.

But Kevin was not here, was not here to control the madness. And within a hot minute the carriage had descended into a chaos. Weary commuters heckled the passing ticket inspector whilst furiously checking their Twitter feeds for updates. The inspector made a run for it.

Finally there was an announcement. '*Signal Failure.*'

The carriage erupted into a chorus of sarcastic cheers, and the once anonymous travelling companions shook heads at each other. Dunkirk Spirit had finally invaded carriage H at 8:35 p.m. on a Monday evening. And Ruby and Gary looked each other and burst out laughing.

8:45 p.m.

The train sat, ticking and cooling. Gary was sipping on his beer and looking at something in the near distance. Ruby was scrolling through her phone log. Five missed calls. Mum.

She took a deep breath, knowing full well why her family were so eager to get hold of her that night.

She placed the phone back in her bag and attempted to distract herself.

'So what's the day job Mr Gary?' she asked half-seriously.

Gary took a final swig of the beer can. His face softened as he responded. 'Carer luv, doing my best for the old folks.'

Ruby was taken aback. This was 180 degrees away from what she'd expected. So he had an altruistic side after all. Not bad for a yob, she thought. She felt conflicted. She rested her head against the train window and surveyed the scene outside. Men in high viz jackets, floodlights and the ever-familiar Ingatestone Hall Level Crossing.

Gary shook the now empty beer can. He cleared his throat. 'And Ruby. What's your gig?'

Ruby shook her head, mainly to herself, and laughed, mainly to herself, and then she looked up and fixed Gary in the eye. 'I'm a psychotherapist specialising in cognitive behavioural therapy, Gary. I do a lot of work with people who've had trauma. PTSD. Ex forces mainly.'

Gary nodded - a tacit gesture of approval. 'OK, *that* is cool' he thought, clearly impressed.

He suddenly noticed that she was also quite attractive, even if she did insist on wearing that rag on her head.

And then the train shuddered to a start. The passengers of the night became a group of faceless commuters once more as they turned their attentions back to their phones, laptops and newspapers,

'Going back to our previous subject, hijab...' Ruby rummaged around in her Michael Kors Selma 2015 edition handbag and took out her phone.

She leant over the table, now full of plastic cups and empty beer cans, and showed Gary a meme she'd posted that very afternoon on her Facebook wall. 'See? A lady without hijab is like an unwrapped toffee apple. Which gets messy and attracts flies.' Sure enough, the meme showed a chastely wrapped toffee apple, and next to it, an unwrapped one, covered in flies.

'Hah!' she said and sat back with a triumphant look.

But Gary's face had dropped as he'd seen her full name. Finally he leant back too, arm across the chair next to him, his face breaking into a smile. 'Bloody hell woman.'

Ruby narrowed her eyes. 'What, Gary. WHAT?'

'It's Ruby *Akram* isn't it? And here's me thinking you were a Facebook avatar...'

In an instant, Ruby realised that they'd been debating regularly on Facebook for the past nine months, on several discussion groups, and that it had descended into bitter acrimony and bad language. Great. Just great, she thought to herself. 'Well, this is awkward', she said to him, and tailed off.

And with a glint of an eye Gary piped up. 'Well that you shut you up didn't it. I'm going to get a beer. Want anything from the bar?'

'Surprise me', Ruby said. He grinned and left and she went back to her copy of the Independent, more as a shield from everyone looking at them than anything else. She shook her head and smiled. Well, this was strange.

Gary got to the front of the queue at the train bar in carriage H and thought about his new; or old, if social media was anything to go by, acquaintance.

Bloody *hell*. This was fucking weird. They'd been shouting at each other for nearly a year; or at least a hijabi with her face turned away from the camera and a scarfed-up football hooligan had. Hah.

He wondered how to talk in front of her when he went back. And he couldn't think of anything. He ordered a can of beer, a bottle of orange juice and a bag of Haribos, paid via contactless, and made his way back, walking like a sailor in a ship against the cradling rocking of the carriages.

Meanwhile Ruby fielded one more dropped call from her mother, and a voicemail, and a text.

'Ruby. Where are you?'

'On a train, mum.'

'When are you back?'

'Soon, mum, soon.'

'Did you get my message about the invite?'

'YES, mother.' Sheesh.

Gary returned from the bar and plunked back down in his seat opposite Ruby. He cracked the ringpull on his can of beer and then passed over a little bottle of orange juice to her.

She smiled. 'Thank you.'

And then he thumped the bag of Haribos onto the table and ripped it open. 'Got these for both of us. Dig in.'

'Can't, Gary. They're haram.'

'Oh fucking hell Ruby. Is everything haram to you lot?'

She narrowed her eyes at him. '"Our lot". Yes. They're haram. They contain gelatine. Which has pig fat. And you swear a lot Gary. You need to learn some adhab.'

Gary sipped from his can, put it down, picked up a Haribo sweet and inspected it. 'Pig fat, huh. Well, I never knew that. And I'm sorry.'

Ruby just looked at him.

Gary put the sweet back in the packet and spoke again. 'Adhab. Sounds familiar. Go on, remind me.'

'Manners, Gary.'

He clicked his fingers. 'Make a good Muslim! I know this one.'

She blinked. 'You do?'

'I do. Went to a talk by Manwar Ali and that was all it was about. Confused the shit out of the kids from the Islamic Society. They'd all turned out thinking they were gonna hear a talk about jihad.'

Ruby laughed and cracked the screwcap on the bottle of orange juice.

And finally, after what had seemed like a fortnight, the train slowed and chugged into Chelmsford.

'And this is me,' said Gary. He stood, and Ruby stood, surprising herself, and they shook hands.

'See you on the usual?' he said. She narrowed her eyes. 'This life follows you, Gary, for better or worse.'

The train wheezed to a stop and the other passengers looked at them.

'Better or worse?' said Gary, and held onto her hand.

She looked up at him, between the plastic tables. 'Better or worse? On here? Oh, we probably shall,' she replied. She wondered whether he meant a train or social media and left it hanging. 'We probably shall. Goodbye Gary.'

'How do you lot say it? Goodbye I mean.'

'Waleykum salaam.'

He grinned, let go of her hand, and left. She sat back down at her table and smiled.

And as the train pulled out of Chelmsford station he walked alongside the windows, tapped at them, and mouthed 'waleykum salaam' at her, and walked away down the platform. She laughed out loud and the rest of the carriage looked at her.

'What?' she said. And she shook her head and went back to her copy of the Independent.

*****

ABOUT THE AUTHORS

Essex kids ***CHARLIE FLOWERS*** *and* ***HANNAH HAQ*** *have been getting up to no good for years, be it impersonating random childrens' parents at school evenings, upsetting people at the opera, or just generally being bad Muslims. So it was only a matter of time before they started writing about what they have seen and the people they've encountered. This is their first short story. But not the last, oh no. Readers can follow their escapades via the hashtags: #flaq #flaqontour #thecurseofflaq*

ABOUT **READERS CIRCLE OF AVENUE PARK**

Are you an active reader who cherishes the written word?

We are too. The READERS' CIRCLE of AVENUE PARK is a book forum founded by readers, for fellow readers, who wish to share in the celebration of all things book-related. Jam-packed with insights and articles about books and the people who write them, from edgy self-published authors with "Indie Cred" to literary giants that grace the best seller lists.

Our mission is to scour the globe searching out intriguing literature. Our readers live everywhere—Great Britain, France, Australia, Canada, United States, South Africa, Ukraine and many places in between. We showcase the most gripping stories we've encountered—books that enthral, engage, allow us to laugh and weep, and finally breathe out a meaningful "Wow!"

We share our favorite books and authors with each other, and make special recommendations for book clubs. In fact, consider #RCAP your personal virtual book club. We are delighted to welcome you to our dynamic fellowship of global readers.

Please join us at www.readersaveneupark.weebly.com -- It is absolutely FREE.

Follow us on Twitter: @ReadersAvenuePark or hashtag #RCAP

Made in the USA
Middletown, DE
08 April 2017